Silliness brought giggles from Davis.

Shaking his head from side to side, he covered his mouth with a sticky hand.

Nash pretended affront. "What? Don't you like Larry, the lasagna?"

"He's not lasagna. He's a 'cumber."

Nash glanced at Harlow for clarification. "'Cumber?"

"Cucumber," she said, smiling. Not at Nash. At her son's adorable language. Though she had to admit her eyes were on the handsome athlete filling up her kitchen.

"How did I not know that?" He grinned back at her, and in spite of her reservations, Harlow started to relax a tiny bit.

Nothing in Nash's demeanor seemed suspicious as he continued to engage Davis—and her—in completely innocent discussions. His charm worked on children as well as it did on women and the press.

If he wondered, even a little, where this sweet-faced boy had come from, he showed no indication of curiosity.

Or was he simply too polite to ask in front of a child?

And was she willing to lie about Davis's parentage and claim another man had fathered the boy?

Linda Goodnight, a *New York Times* bestselling author and winner of a RITA® Award in inspirational fiction, has appeared on the Christian bestseller list. Her novels have been translated into more than a dozen languages. Active in orphan ministry, Linda enjoys writing fiction that carries a message of hope in a sometimes dark world. She and her husband live in Oklahoma. Visit her website, lindagoodnight.com, for more information.

Books by Linda Goodnight

Love Inspired

Sundown Valley

To Protect His Children
Keeping Them Safe
The Cowboy's Journey Home
Her Secret Son

The Buchanons

Cowboy Under the Mistletoe
The Christmas Family
Lone Star Dad
Lone Star Bachelor

Love Inspired Trade

Claiming Her Legacy

Visit the Author Profile page at LoveInspired.com for more titles.

Her Secret Son

Linda Goodnight

ISBN-13: 978-1-335-58611-7

Her Secret Son

For questions and comments about the quality of this book, please contact us at CustomerService@Harlequin.com.

Love Inspired
22 Adelaide St. West, 41st Floor
Toronto, Ontario M5H 4E3, Canada
www.LoveInspired.com

Printed in U.S.A.

For the love of money is the root of all evil:
which while some coveted after, they have erred
from the faith, and pierced themselves through
with many sorrows.

—*1 Timothy* 6:10

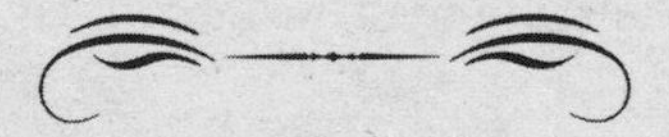

In memory of my mother,
whose unusual cheekbone dimple inspired the idea for little Davis. She would be delighted to know that her dimple has finally made a reappearance, not only in this book, but on the face of her great-grandson, Luke Travis.
Wish she was here to see it.

Chapter One

Cold, wet and weary, Harlow Matheson slouched low in the saddle and let Burr have his tawny equine head across the south pasture of Matheson Ranch. Days like this she wondered why she fought so hard to keep the two hundred acres of dirt and grass afloat.

If she didn't miss her guess, the sun was up there somewhere, scurrying toward the horizon to escape the downpour. She wouldn't be able see it even if she looked. The prongs of icy rain from bruised, swollen skies battered her, her horse, the earth.

Somewhere a mama cow, number twenty-eight, was giving birth. Finding her and her hapless offspring in this monsoon meant finding a pile of money Harlow couldn't afford to lose.

If her sister Monroe wasn't laid up with a broken leg, there would be another rider to search the timberline and creek banks. Poppy couldn't. Not in this weather. Not anymore. Matheson Ranch was Harlow's responsibility now. So was her family. All of them. Even the one who'd run away. Maybe her more than the ones who'd stayed.

Harlow sighed into the howling rain.

Could a twenty-four-year-old run away?

Technically, no, but Taylor's leaving felt like running away to her sisters.

Harlow was the eldest, the one who'd practically raised Taylor. How could the girl just leave?

The ache that was her baby sister lingered, although the immediacy of the weather and a cow and calf in trouble demanded Harlow's full attention.

Rain fell in sheets now, a toad-strangler, Poppy would say. Or maybe a gully-washer. Her grandpa had a saying for everything.

Using only her legs to guide Burr, she angled him toward the east and the acres of tangled woods, green briars and belly-high brush. She couldn't see the trees for the heavy rain, but she knew where they were. She and Burr detested searching the dense, brushy, thorn-invested area, but it was the most likely place for a cow to shelter while in labor—as long as the creek didn't rise and drown both mama cow and baby.

"Heifers always wait until the worst weather." Another of Poppy's maxims. "Then they go off and hide from you."

He was right. Poppy was always right about critters. It was people who fooled him.

Harlow shivered, chilled to the bone, rain sluicing down her face. She'd braided her hair in defense against the onslaught of rain and whipping wind. Water dripped from the dark red tips, a waist-length stream of hair as ruddy as the North Canadian River. Her Stetson over hoodie provided meager protection, the brim forming a waterfall that obscured her vision.

It was because of this rain blindness that she almost missed him, the lone rider a hundred yards away coming down the rise. He was bent low over the saddle, his nose bobbing dangerously close to the saddle horn.

Harlow slashed a hand across her soaked face and squinted, but the pounding rain came right back at her. She shook her head, heard the slosh and slap of braids against the sides of her face.

Something about the way the rider sat the horse warned her. Something was wrong.

Nash Corbin figured he was about to die. He couldn't hold on much longer. Truth be told, the dark, soggy ground looked almost welcoming. He was that exhausted. The pain was getting worse. And his arms grew weaker with each stride his horse took.

He could let go of the saddle horn. His body wouldn't hold him up any longer and he'd tumble to the earth. Maybe he would. Just let go. Be done with it.

He desperately needed to lie down.

In a day or two when the rains eased, some random soul would find him, facedown in the mud. Didn't most legends end that way? Dead and alone in some unsavory circumstance?

Not that he'd reached legend status, but news of his death would make the papers and all the sports talk shows.

He should have told someone where he was headed, but no, in his anger and hurt, he'd gone rogue, tossed his cell phone in a drawer, jumped in his Corvette and rocketed to the Oklahoma ranch no one in his current life knew existed except him. Not even his agent. *Especially* his agent.

The sharp pain tore into him again. He had no energy left to fight the agonized groan. Normally, he'd have held in the sound, but not this time. He let the cry rip from deep in his chest, a shout of pain and despair. No one would hear him anyway.

The deluge, coming down in sideways sheets, filled his opened mouth. He shut it. Shivered. Wondered where he was. He couldn't be far from his ranch house. Unless he'd chosen the wrong direction. Which wouldn't surprise him in the least.

He'd chosen the wrong direction a lot lately, in more ways than one.

Even Drifter seemed confused about their location. The dependable black horse plodded, head down, as tired and depressed as his rider.

Neither of them could see in this downpour.

How far had he ridden, wild and furious and

trying to figure out how he'd let his life get so out of control? He had no idea.

And as if God really wanted to punish him, while roaming the woods and fields, his head in a very bad place, rain increasing by the moment, Nash was suddenly attacked with the worse belly pain in memory.

His coach would croak if he had the slightest inkling that his star receiver and Super Bowl MVP was about to fall from a horse, bust up his other shoulder and die in the mud. The cash cow was in bad enough shape as it was.

Nash's forehead bobbed against the saddle horn. Once, twice. He tried to sit up straight but the pain struck again, a rip, a tear. Worse than the torn rotator cuff. Bad enough to make a lesser man cry. But big, tough pros didn't cry. They played hurt. They played sick. They played, no matter the rain or snow or bitter cold.

Nash Corbin had played until his body couldn't take it anymore.

He heard the roar of the Sunday crowd, the sound of money, the fame and the sheer thrill of victory, and remembered his mother's admonition to attend church before every game.

He hadn't. He'd been having too much fun being rich and famous.

"Sorry, Mom," he moaned.

Her face appeared before him, the familiar

dimple at the very top of her left cheekbone, her green eyes worried.

No, it couldn't be Mom. Mom was overseas. Dad was gone. No one was left in this entire country but him and Drifter and a pack of hangers-on who'd leave the moment they discovered he was broke. Social media would go berserk. Probably already had after he'd disappeared without a word, but he was too out of touch to know.

Despair slammed him with the next pain, and even if he'd wanted to, he could hold on no longer.

Nash Corbin, the iron man who'd never passed out during a game no matter the injury, let the darkness overtake him.

With wind tearing at the tails of her slicker and threatening to dislodge her hat, Harlow dipped her chin and rode hard, urging Burr to a dangerous speed in this slush and mush. The sturdy cow pony responded with courage. His hooves made sucking noises in the mud.

As she approached the other rider, the man—for she was pretty sure by his size that he was male—slipped sideways in the saddle. Splayed hands holding nothing but air, he started down. It was a long way to the ground, and a hard fall, no matter how soft the mud below.

If he went down, she wouldn't be able to get him back on the horse without help.

And *he* didn't look capable of helping with anything.

Quickly sidling Burr alongside the muscular black horse, Harlow reached out to brace the other rider's near shoulder. She gave a hefty shove.

A deep, agonized groan slid through the man's rain-drenched lips. Harlow pushed anyway, her slight form barely able to hold him steady. She was strong for her size, had to be. She regularly wrestled calves into chutes and forced bawling cows to their feet. But, like his horse, this man was tall, wide, just plain big.

"Hey!" she shouted against the rain. "Are you okay?"

Silly question. He was as limp as a hot noodle, and the agonized cry had to mean something. "What's wrong? Can you talk?"

His answer, above the deafening downpour, was silence.

Harlow closed her eyes for the briefest of moments. The calf she sought could drown, and if the cow was down, she could die too. Saving them both meant money in the bank. She desperately needed that money.

Her conscience pecked, and the decision was made. A human in jeopardy trumped money any day of the week.

"Help me, Lord," she murmured, tasting the cold rain with every movement. "Okay, big guy, we gotta get you out of this weather. I'm gonna tie you on the saddle. Don't fight me."

As if he could.

With the well-trained Burr instinctively knowing when to remain still, Harlow jerked the lariat rope from her saddle horn and tossed it around the man before sliding to the boggy earth. Her boots sank to the ankle. She'd worked with enough struggling calves to be quick, and she tied the big man to both horse and saddle, his face down against the saddle horn. At least, he wouldn't drown.

Something about him seemed familiar—too familiar—and the skin crawled on the back of her neck. But he couldn't be Nash. No matter how wide his shoulders or how tall he was. If it was Nash, she'd leave him here, let him hit the ground and drown himself.

Her conscience tweaked louder, that pesky thing. Ever since giving her life to Jesus three years ago, she'd been determined to do the right thing even if it cost her.

If this guy was Nash Corbin, it likely would. He'd already cost her plenty.

"Sorry," she whispered against the rain.

The Lord had forgiven her for a lot of mistakes. She didn't want to let Him down anymore, even if it meant seeing Nash Corbin again.

In a useless gesture, she slung the rain from her hat, then clapped it back in place. The sick man was bareheaded, his hair so wet she couldn't determine the color.

Nash's hair was a rich chestnut brown. He had the kind of hair and face and physique that attracted women like bees to the hive. Back in the day, he'd been mostly oblivious, too focused on football, his ticket out of Sundown Valley and the ranch life he despised.

Not that she wanted to remember anything about the man who'd once been her best buddy.

Some buddy he'd turned out to be.

Please, God, don't let this be Nash.

She considered removing her slicker and covering him with it. The fool had ridden out into this mess in nothing but a windbreaker, which was soaked through. It did, however, have a hood, so she tugged it up and fished beneath his chin for the ties. Her hand froze. For there, on his thickly muscled neck, was a small, round, keloid scar. Exactly like the one Nash had.

His skin was warmth to her chill. She jerked her hand away.

Oh, Jesus. Oh, Jesus. The words were a prayer.

It was him. Nash Corbin. The one man she never wanted to see again. Couldn't bear to see.

What was he doing *here* on her land? And why? When he'd left, he'd sworn never to set foot on a ranch, or in this town, again.

He'd kept that promise. Until now.

He groaned again, and Harlow sprang into action. Nash or not, he needed help. He'd be sicker if she didn't do something quick.

Hoping the man was secured enough to travel, Harlow gathered the black horse's reins in one hand, hopped onto Burr and started the long trek back to the house.

What would her family say when they discovered she'd brought the enemy to their doorstep?

But she knew, at least about her grandpa. Poppy would do the right thing. He always did. Poppy's code of ethics was soul deep and too full of Jesus to do anything less. It was Nash who didn't know the meaning of right or honor or ethics. He'd wanted to be rich and hadn't cared who he hurt to get there. The dirty, rotten, lowdown scoundrel.

Harlow set her teeth, stomach churning, and mind abuzz with questions and worries about things she didn't want to think about or consider.

Nash. Why now? Nearly four years had passed and not once had he returned to his family home. The formerly vibrant Corbin Ranch sat sad and abandoned on eighty acres of what was now weeds and saplings. The lawn had gone unmowed, the hay uncut, the buildings left to the mice and birds and wasps.

Through newly formed streams and standing water, down ravines and up the other side Harlow rode, leading the black horse. All the while, she kept a watchful eye on the man bobbing loosely in the saddle like the dead.

Harlow shivered as much from the ugly thought as from the cold rain. She didn't hate Nash Corbin. Didn't wish him dead. She did, however, wish him gone.

Chapter Two

Thunder rumbled from the west and lightning ripped the darkened sky. The storm was worsening, especially the one inside Harlow.

The momentary flash of light displayed the hazy shape of a two-story house and a smatter of outbuildings. Home, at last. Home and warmth.

And a family who would be shocked out of their heads.

She glanced over one shoulder. Nash and his horse were barely visible in the downpour even though she held the black's reins and he was only a few feet away from Burr's tail. She snugged him closer, drawing him alongside Burr as she urged her mount toward the front gate.

Leaning down, she flipped up the latch, grateful it didn't stick this time, and rode across the soggy yard and onto the low-slung wooden porch. Although the rain ceased beneath the porch roof, and should have been a relief, the pounding on the tin structure increased Harlow's anxiety about the cattle she had not been able to find.

The calf would likely drown in this deluge. She hoped the cow didn't.

If God was watching, she wondered if He'd give her credit for saving Nash Corbin's worthless carcass and, in reward, protect the cow-calf pair. The animals were a lot more valuable to the Matheson family than this troublesome lump of humanity.

Dismounting, she raked the sopping hat from her head and tossed it onto one of the Adirondack chairs lining the long front porch. Water fell like Niagara from the roof, creating a curtain of rain that splashed onto the porch and ran in streams between the plywood boards.

Her sick neighbor, for she wouldn't call him a friend, rcmained silent and still, though a quick touch of his neck and that telltale keloid scar let her know he was alive. Passed out, she supposed, from whatever malady assailed him.

What had possessed him to be riding through her pasture in this rainstorm anyway? Had he been seeking help because he was sick? Why was he back in the area in the first place? He'd never come home before.

With an annoyed grunt, Harlow squeezed as much water from her clothes and hair as she could and tried to focus on the main problem.

Nash's reasons for doing anything were not her concern. He'd made that clear four years ago.

Getting him on his feet and back where he belonged before he caused more disaster for her family was all that mattered.

She shoved open the front door.

Ollie, the family collie, jumped to her feet and yipped her usual greeting.

"Monroe. Poppy!" Harlow leaned into the house without entering and shouted over the dog. She dripped puddles onto the tile entryway. "I need help."

The dog trotted around Harlow and out onto the porch to sniff the strange horse and the man's dangling legs. Thunder boomed and she darted back inside. Ollie was a good cow dog but, unlike her owner, she refused to work in a thunderstorm.

Harlow couldn't blame her.

Leaning heavily on his cane, Poppy hobbled around the opening that led from the living area into the kitchen. His speed was impaired by knees that needed replacing and hips that probably did too. Another ongoing concern for which Harlow had neither answer nor money. God would provide. That's what Poppy always said. Harlow sure wished the Almighty would hurry.

"What's wrong?" Her grandpa's weathered face showed alarm, his snowy eyebrows arched high on his forehead.

Harlow was not one to panic. She rarely asked

for help. The fact that she sounded breathless and upset would scare the whole family. But she couldn't help it. Nash raised all sorts of fears inside her.

To her left, Monroe thumped down the stairs on crutches at breakneck speed with the same troubled expression on her face. A frown pulled at the facial scars she tried to hide behind long, luxurious blond hair.

"Are you hurt? What is it?" Monroe demanded in that no-nonsense staccato of hers.

Affection filled Harlow's chest, pushing out some of the anxiety from discovering Nash Corbin half-dead on her property.

These two, a wounded-warrior sister and a crippled, aging grandfather, both in pain, would fight a bear for her, damaged legs and all.

She felt the same. Which was exactly why Nash's presence disturbed her so much.

He'd hurt them, every single one of them, and had never had enough character to even apologize, much less fix the problem.

Not that she wanted anything from him *now*.

"I'm okay. Just soaked to the bone," she said. "But there's a sick man on the front porch."

"A man?" Monroe's lips curled in distaste, as if she'd sucked a sour lemon. Men, other than Poppy and Davis, were not her favorite species.

"He needs help." She didn't mention who the man was. They'd know soon enough. "I spotted him riding across our land just about the time he started falling from his horse. He's in a bad way."

By now Poppy had reached the front door and pushed out onto the porch. Over one shoulder, he hollered, "Let's get him in. He'll catch epizooti out here in this sod-soaker."

Epizooti was Poppy's word for any illness he couldn't name. Which was most of them.

"Who is he? What was he doing in our pasture?" Monroe demanded from midway across the small living room, as if she'd let the man drown unless he met with her approval.

Which he most definitely wouldn't.

"I'm afraid to tell you. Just get a sheet or something we can use to drag him. When I found him, he was only half-conscious and groaning like a sick bull." Harlow spun and headed back out the door, leaving explanations for later.

Nash, still lashed to the saddle like a side of bacon, hadn't moved. Poppy's white handlebar mustache worked up and down. He was gnawing on something, probably a thought.

"Horse looks familiar." He nodded. Smacked his lips. "Yep. I know this horse."

Of course he did. She should have recognized him, too. Every time she'd driven past Ike Crowder's pasture, the horse was a reminder she didn't want. She'd always wondered why Nash hadn't sold him outright instead of boarding him with a neighboring ranch.

Harlow didn't say any of this. Poppy and Monroe would both know soon enough that she'd brought the worst possible person in out of the rain. Poppy wouldn't shoot him, but Monroe might. But then, her sister knew a lot more about Nash Corbin than Poppy did. And Poppy knew plenty.

As she untied Nash from the saddle, Harlow shivered, both from the wet chill and the worry about what might happen in the next few minutes. She had to get him on his feet and out of here as soon as possible. Like yesterday.

Why. Was. He. Here?

Monroe thumped out the door, a wadded sheet in hand. Leaning her underarms on her crutches, she used both hands to spread the sheet onto the porch. It was instantly soaked. But then, so was the man.

While Monroe held the big horse still, Harlow and Poppy eased the patient onto the sheet. He flopped onto his back and muttered incoherently.

Monroe gave a squeak, quickly squelched as her gaze flew to meet her sister's. Harlow shook her head slightly, a warning to say nothing in front of Poppy.

"I declare, girls," Poppy said, his breath puffing short from the exertion. "That's the Corbin boy."

"Call the cops," Monroe grumbled.

"Now, little gal, that's not a Christian thing

to say. Hc needs help and we'll give it. God forgives. So can we."

Monroe's face closed up like a miser's purse strings, but she was too respectful to argue with the man who'd taken in three little girls when he didn't have to.

But she flashed Harlow a warning glare anyway.

Harlow knew she was playing with fire by letting this man inside her home, but Poppy was right. Since becoming a Christian, she tried hard to follow the teachings of Jesus. He always helped those in need, even when others questioned His common sense.

She was definitely questioning hers right now.

Her nerves jittered as she and her hobble-legged family dragged a groaning, moaning Nash Corbin across the porch, over the bumpy threshold and into their living room.

Settling him on the rug nearest the furnace, the three stared down at his now inert body.

She'd forgotten how big hc was.

"He needs out of those wet clothes," Poppy said.

Monroe scoffed. "That's not happening. I'll get some blankets and towels." She started forward then stopped to fire one more death-ray glare at Nash. "But I'd rather drag him back outside and let him drown."

Poppy offered Monroe one of his warning

glances, the kind he'd used on all three girls when they'd misbehaved as kids.

"Now, sis, look at the boy. He's as pitiful as a motherless calf. Green around the gills, all fevered and puny."

Poppy was a master at mixing metaphors, which usually made Harlow laugh. Except there was nothing humorous about having a sick, soaked Nash Corbin sprawled like a giant rag doll on their rug.

Harlow knelt beside the makeshift pallet. Quelling the apprehension building like a bonfire inside her, she placed a hand to Nash's forehead.

"He's burning with fever and unconscious. I think we should call an ambulance." Get him out of here fast.

She started to rise to do exactly that.

Powerfully strong fingers shot out and gripped her wrist.

"No. No one knows I'm here. No publicity."

Disgust curdled in Harlow's chest.

Nash was awake. And thinking about publicity.

She rolled her eyes. Big-shot superstar was afraid his fans would chase him down and see him in less than superstar condition. Or maybe he was worried about some woman he'd jilted coming after him.

She didn't like thinking those things, but there they were. He was still the best-looking man she'd ever known. Naturally, his successful football career had made those looks popular with lots of females. The last time she'd checked, he had over a million followers on social media.

Yes, foolish as it was, she'd looked.

But she had *not* followed him. She hadn't gone after him four years ago, and she sure wouldn't now.

She'd stood by her decision not to ever contact him, not to ask him for anything, though he owed her plenty.

If he'd cared, if she'd mattered, he would have contacted her beyond the two measly phone calls he'd made the week after he left for the big time.

He hadn't. He'd sent his creep of an agent instead, and look how that turned out.

"You're sick, Nash. You should go to the emergency room."

He struggled to sit up, but failed, wincing with every movement while cradling his right arm.

The effort left him breathless and grunting in pain. But at least he was awake and able to move. She sure didn't want him dying in her living room.

"Something I ate. Be okay in a minute." He grunted on every word.

Expression tight with obvious distress, he curved his body inward and stopped attempting to rise.

"Don't want anyone to know I'm here."

"I got that part," Harlow said, her tone a tad testy. "We all did."

A sound on the stairs jerked her attention upward. Her heart stopped.

No. No. No.

"Mommy?"

Her gaze shot from the little boy peering through the railing to her sister who looked as deer-in-the-headlights as Harlow felt.

Why, why, why, did Davis have to wake up from his nap now?

Help me, Jesus.

She swallowed a lump of terror, trying to think what to do and praying Nash was too sick to notice a small child on the steps.

As if her sister could read her mind, Monroe sprang into action, as fast as a woman on crutches and in an enormous leg cast could spring.

"What is it, baby?" Monroe thumped toward the bottom of the staircase and looked up at Davis. "Do you want a snack?"

Rubbing his eyes, the three-year-old nodded. "I hungy."

"Isn't he supposed to be napping?" Harlow asked from her spot kneeling beside the sick football player. His eyes were closed. Hopefully, he'd passed out again.

Monroe picked up on the desperate cue.

"Go back to your room, Davis, honey, and I'll bring you some juice. Okay?"

"And amanal cwackers?" he asked, apparently

more interested in a snack than in the stranger moaning on the living room rug.

But then, a calf in the living room wasn't that unusual. To a three-year-old, she supposed a man wasn't that much different.

"You got it, buddy." Monroe made a shooing motion with one crutch. "Now, scoot."

With the giggle that inevitably filled Harlow's chest with pleasure, Davis hunched his little shoulders and returned the way he'd come.

Monroe was savvy enough not to look at Harlow as she and her crutches thudded toward the kitchen to collect the promised snack.

Harlow slowly released her breath, though her pulse ricocheted all over the place. Nash was apparently too sick to notice the boy. He'd never even opened his eyes.

Disaster averted.

For now.

But if Nash stuck around her living room floor much longer, Davis would finish his snack and find his way back downstairs.

The man. Had. To. Go. *Now.*

"Nash." She gently shook his shoulder. "Nash."

He winced, curled away from her hand and made a mumbling noise that said he was listening. Sort of.

"You can't stay here, Nash. You need more help than we can give. You need a doctor."

How did she sound so calm when her heart raced and her mouth was drier than cotton?

Suddenly, Nash's eyes flew open. He bolted upright and leaned forward, panting. "I'm going to be sick."

"He's green as frog soup," Poppy yelped. "Get him up."

Somehow, with Harlow's help, Nash managed to struggle to his feet and then stumble toward the bathroom.

She was amazed he remembered where it was. He'd forgotten everything else about this town and his friends when he'd hit the big time.

"I'll bring the truck around," Poppy said, already clapping the floppy, flat-brimmed felt on top of his white head. "That boy needs to see a doctor, and I'm taking him whether he likes it or not." He huffed, "*Pshaw*. Publicity."

"I'll bring the truck around, Poppy," Harlow said. "I'm already drenched."

"I said I'll get the truck and I aim to. Rain's letting up." He gave her that belligerent look that said he suspected she was coddling him. "I'm old but I'm not helpless. You go get those clothes changed before you catch your death. I'll handle this fella."

When he talked like that she didn't argue. Lately, she walked a tightrope to balance Poppy's pride against his well-being. A little rain wouldn't hurt him. Hopefully.

She sure didn't want *him* catching epizooti.

After Poppy left the house, Monroe, standing at the foot of the stairs with Davis's snack in hand, glanced toward the bathroom before hissing, "What are you going to do? You can't let that lowlife, no-good, cheating, lying buzzard anywhere near Davis. Or us, for that matter."

She already had.

"I know that, Monroe," she whispered back. "I don't like him any more than you do, but what choice do I have? He's here. He's sick. As much as our family despises what he did to do us, I'm not adding any more heartache to Poppy by telling him the rest of Nash's betrayal. He'd be devastated. Again."

"And he'd go after Nash with a shotgun, insisting he man up and marry you."

"Trust me. I remember when he first learned I was pregnant. He promised to make the guilty party act like a man and do right by me. All I had to do was name the guy."

"Which you refused to do."

"You know why. Nash and I were never a couple. No matter that I'd been in love with him all my life, he considered me as only a friend. He'd just accomplished the dream of a lifetime. He would have despised me if I'd ruined that for him."

"Maybe. But maybe he'd have stepped up and taken care of you and Davis."

"I didn't want him to 'step up.'" She put the words in air quotes. "I wanted him to—"

Monroe put a hand on her shoulder. "You wanted love and romance and all that nonsense."

"It's not nonsense to want to be loved, even now that I've given up hope of that ever happening."

Sad-eyed, Monroe shook her head. "Love hurts more than it feels good. I never want to feel that kind of grief again, and I don't want that for you either."

Harlow hugged her sister's shoulders. Monroe had fallen hard for a military man, had followed him into the navy. But her Prince Charming had turned out to be a frog.

So had Nash, though he'd never known Harlow was in love with him. Monroe's man had known, and he'd shattered her heart, her confidence and her career.

"This conversation isn't about me and my bad choices." Monroe pointed one of her crutches toward the closed bathroom door. "What are you going to do about *him*?"

"I don't know yet."

"If you don't want Nash discovering the truth about Davis and making demands that his money can buy and ours can't fight, you'd better think fast."

"He wouldn't take Davis. He never wanted him."

"You don't know that."

True.

But he hadn't wanted her. Why would he want their child?

Her conscience tugged for the first time in a long time. The old Nash, the boy she'd fallen for in high school who'd never considered her anything more than a friend, was a good guy. He'd been honest with her about his intentions. He'd even called to ask if she was okay and to apologize for what had happened.

She hadn't known then that she was pregnant, but Nash's apology still lingered, bittersweet, in her heart.

He'd been sorry. He'd had big plans. And they had not included her or a baby.

She could have forgiven him for that.

But this guy wasn't that sweet old Nash. This was the scoundrel who'd cheated them all without so much as a flinch. He was Mr. Superstar with a million fans and even more money. A superstar who avoided publicity.

Double ugh.

Harlow put a hand to her forehead. Her brain hurt. Nash Corbin had broken her heart and driven her family to the edge of bankruptcy.

But he'd also given her the greatest gift of her life. He'd given her Davis.

Chapter Three

Nash leaned his head against the cool passenger window of Gus Matheson's pickup truck. He was shivering, burning with fever, and his guts felt like he'd been stomped by a three-hundred-pound lineman wearing spikes.

"Take me to my place, Gus," he managed to say between waves of nausea. "I'm better."

Gus cast a quick glance at him and grunted. "You don't look better."

Nash would have grinned if he hadn't hurt so bad. The grizzled old rancher he'd known all his life hadn't changed one iota. He was honest to the bone and good to the soul, a man who practiced what he preached. But he was also a gruff straight shooter.

Gus was right. He felt as bad as he looked. Thankfully, at the moment, he was upright. Sort of. The door was doing a pretty good job of holding him in place.

"Something I ate." He had no idea if that was true or not.

"What? Rotten alligator?"

"A live one, gnawing his way out."

Gus chuckled, as Nash had intended. "I don't mind driving you to the ER. You sure you'll be okay over at your ranch all alone?"

No. "Yes."

Gus glanced in his direction, then back to the muddy, potholed country road. Rain started to splat the windshield again. "You got one of them team doctors, don't you?"

"Sure." He tilted forward, holding his belly and hoping the short, but inhumanely bumpy ride between the Matheson Ranch and his own didn't make him throw up again. To be on the safe side, he rolled down the window. Never mind the rain. He was already soaked. "I'll call him."

Not today. Maybe not tomorrow. But eventually.

"All right then. If you're certain." Gus turned the steering wheel and rattled over the long, weed-choked, puddle-filled driveway leading to Nash's ranch house. The small brick structure had never been much. It was less now.

Beneath the leaning carport, his snazzy red sports car looked ridiculously out of place. Soon, he'd be on foot, the car repossessed unless he could figure out something fast.

Right now, he was too sick to live, much less care.

Gus pulled the pickup as close to the front door as possible and turned, one wiry, slicker-clad arm atop the steering wheel. He settled his wise gaze on Nash.

Nash hoped the older man didn't see too much with those experienced eyes of his. He was too embarrassed to let anyone know the kind of mistakes he'd made.

"A right blessing Harlow found you when she did," the older man said, his tone gentle. "God was looking out for you, boy. No matter what you've done, He cares."

Nash was too sick to question exactly what Gus meant by the comment. He hadn't lived a holy life in the last four years, but he wasn't the Hollywood partying type either. He was too focused on making money.

Which he no longer had. Thanks to his unscrupulous agent, a man he'd trusted with everything.

Every little thing he owned.

Except for this falling down ranch.

A groan that had little to do with his belly pain slid through his lips.

He'd been a fool. A green kid with stars in his eyes and the promise of more money in a year than his dad had eked out of this ranch in a lifetime. The power brokers had made promises, and he'd believed them.

Weak and sick, he couldn't think about that

now. It hurt almost as much as the alligator in his guts.

"Thanks, Gus."

He made a move toward opening the truck door. The mundane activity was harder than it should have been.

"I'll look after your horse 'til you're back on your pegs. You call if you need us."

"Right." He couldn't. He didn't have a phone. Which could prove to be another foolish thing he'd done if this belly pain turned out to be something serious.

He reached for the door handle with his left hand and pushed. The right shoulder couldn't handle the strain.

Sliding to his feet, his knees wobbled worse than the time he'd been blindsided and knocked unconscious in the end zone. He'd hung on to the football, made the touchdown, but he didn't even remember it. The film was too scary to watch more than once. He'd looked dead.

This time he hung on to the side of Gus's flatbed Dodge.

Another pain hit him. He swallowed the cry but froze in place for a good five seconds, waiting, hoping, praying the agony would end.

Gus was not fooled. "You need help, boy? I ain't much, but I can get you in that house."

No, he couldn't. At six feet four inches and 235 pounds, Nash was more than a lot of big men could handle. Gus was a small, wiry guy. And eighty years old.

"I'm good." Except he wasn't. Not that he'd let Gus know it. He'd walk into that house, just as he'd walked off the football field, under his own power unless he passed out.

Which could happen.

He stepped away from the truck and shut the door, though he couldn't stand straight. The house looked a hundred miles away.

Fourth down and fifty yards to go.

Gus stared at him for one more long moment before nodding.

Through the rain peppering his eyelids, Nash nodded his reply.

He wanted to lift a hand and wave, but he required all his energy to put one foot in front of the other and, bent like a boomerang, make his way up the steps and into the house.

As soon as he entered the living room, he collapsed on the couch, his sudden weight releasing a swirl of dust motes. He couldn't ever remember being so relieved to lie down.

If Harlow hadn't come along when she had... He didn't want to think about what might have happened.

He was still depressed, still hurting and half out of it, and definitely still broke, but he was glad to have made it back to the ranch house in one piece.

Thanks to Harlow.

Nash frowned, trying to remember the last hour.

How had he ended up with Harlow?

He saw her again inside his mind, rain dripping from her dark red braid, determination in those hazel eyes of hers.

Harlow. Good old Harlow.

It was the last thought he had for a while.

When he opened his eyes again, the girl next door was also his first thought.

Probably because she'd once been his buddy and he hadn't seen her in a long time.

She'd saved his hide today.

He supposed she had anyway. He was a tad foggy on the details.

He squinted toward the curtained window. Was it still today? Or had he slept into the night?

He didn't know. Or care.

Didn't matter. He wasn't going anywhere.

His head hurt but thankfully, his belly, though testy and aching, wasn't in a paroxysm of agony like before.

Had he weathered the worst?

Or was there more to come?

He should get up, change clothes, hit the bed under warm covers.

Except he couldn't.

His wet jeans and shirt stuck to his skin, as heavy and itchy as wool underwear, and he was cold to the point of shivering, but he couldn't make himself get up.

Soon he'd have to. But not yet.

One hand dangling over the side of the couch; his fingers grazed a throw rug. He managed to pull it up and over his chest and arms.

Better. Not much but some.

The headache pinged against his temples. His foggy, feverish brain ached all the way down his neck and over his injured shoulder.

He closed his eyes. Harlow appeared.

She looked good.

A half grunt, half chuckle made him wince. Harlow had been muddy and soaked to the skin. But he still thought she looked good. Not good in the romantic sense. She looked well. Healthy.

Yeah.

They'd been good friends back in the day, riding horses together, cheering each other on. She'd been as thrilled as anyone when he'd been selected in the second round of the NFL draft.

They both had been.

Their celebration that night had been one of the stupidest things he'd ever done in his life. Another reason he'd become a teetotaler.

Later, he'd made sure Harlow was all right. From the looks of her today, she was more than all right.

His foggy brain drifted around trying to pinpoint something. A tension he'd felt from the Matheson household. No one had seemed too friendly. Especially Harlow.

Probably because she was worried about his sickness. She could be abrupt and testy when worrying over people she cared about.

Harlow was the kind of girl who took care of everyone else before letting herself enjoy life.

Was she enjoying life?

His agent said she was. Said she was dating a nice guy and that her family's ranch was prospering.

He'd been happy for her and for the fine family of neighbors he'd known all his life. They deserved good things to happen.

But that was several years ago. Nash hadn't exactly kept in touch.

He knew the reasons why.

When he'd left this ranch four years ago, he'd shaken the dust off his feet and never planned to chase another cow or stack another barn full of hay. Ranching was not for him. It had nearly ruined his parents, had driven his dad to an early grave, and he'd been determined to get an education and get out.

When he'd been fortunate enough to be both big and talented at football, he'd made up his mind to take advantage of everything the sport had to offer. Especially the money. Always the money.

Then he'd been so caught up in the pressure of making the team, of learning new skills and navigating the world of agents, media, financial success, endorsements, and most of all, his team's expectations, that he'd put his personal life on the back burner.

He hadn't completely forgotten Harlow and the Mathesons, but he'd let them slide into the background. Sterling Dorsey, his agent, claimed that the way to success meant total focus on the game, put everything else in his life in the agent's knowledgeable hands, and leave past baggage behind.

Nash had never considered his friends as baggage, but Sterling knew his business. At least that's what Nash had thought then. He'd been too small-town green and eager to recognize the danger of handing over his whole life, especially his finances, to one man.

Regardless, he should have kept in contact with his neighbors, should have kept up with them.

He'd called once or twice after that wild, reckless night of celebration to be sure Harlow was okay. She claimed she was, and nothing in her cheerful tone led him to believe differently. Still, he'd asked Sterling to check on her a few more times.

Soon, the girl, the ranch, the small Okie town hidden deep in the Kiamichi Mountains faded away in football games, practices, media and the whirlwind of the National Football League. A top athlete had to focus on the sport if he expected to earn a big contract.

His work had paid off.

Until now.

The hammer in his head banged harder until he couldn't think anymore. Didn't want to think. About the financial mess he was in, the damaged shoulder and now this sickness.

And the people he'd left behind in his climb to the top.

As soon as he felt better, he'd drive over to the Matheson Ranch.

Good people. Good friends. Wouldn't hurt to get reacquainted while he figured out the rest of his life.

"We can't let him anywhere near this ranch again." Monroe ground the words out as if she were crushing glass with her molars. "I won't have him upsetting you or Davis or Poppy."

Harlow braced a hand on her sister's shoulder and sat next to her on the twin bed she'd slept in since coming to live with Poppy as a child.

The bed, like the room, was plain and simple. White walls, a small closet, a secondhand nightstand with a pale green-shaded lamp, and a matching green throw rug on the hardwood floor. Other than a photo of her late parents on one wall, she had never bothered to change anything except for adding a bassinet when Davis was born. When he'd grown too big, she'd fretted about letting him sleep in a room by himself. He'd adjusted quicker and better than she had.

"I appreciate that, sis, I really do, but Nash is sick. He's not going anywhere for a while. We'll have to deal with it." Somehow.

"Aren't you worried about what might happen?"

Worried? She was scared out of her mind. And oddly conflicted now that she'd seen him again.

"You know I am. Hopefully, he's only here for a couple of days to recoup from this illness and then he'll leave again."

"Maybe someone from his team or perhaps that awful agent will come and get him." Monroe's mouth twisted. "Or his girlfriend."

Harlow didn't want to think about encountering Nash's latest conquest, especially since she'd been one of them.

"As long as they stay over there and don't bother us, we'll be okay."

"And what if they, meaning *he*, doesn't? What if he gets well, shows up at our door, takes one look at Davis and demands custody? What if Nash takes him back to Florida with him?"

The idea scared her spitless. "Nash wouldn't do that."

"How do you know?"

"He has a career, a new life, the life he dreamed about for years. Besides, Davis doesn't look anything like Nash. I doubt he'd ever guess that Davis is his child."

"I hope you're right. But what if you're not?"

Harlow pushed off the bed and went to the door. Nash was the unresolvable problem. She did not want to talk about this anymore. Preferably ever, though she knew Monroe would not let go of the topic for long.

"I'm going back out to look for that cow."

Monroe squinted at her, not fooled by the swift subject change.

"It'll be dark soon."

"I have a lantern, and Burr is solid in darkness and bad weather. We'll be fine." Opening the door into the hallway, she paused. "Will you start dinner? Make sure Davis eats some of his veggies and gets a bath if I'm out late?"

"You know I will, but there's no point in you going until this rain stops. You won't be able to get across Lost Creek, and that's probably where the cow is."

Harlow's shoulders sagged momentarily, but she yanked them upright again. "I have to try. We can't afford to lose them."

"Some things are out of our hands, Harlow."

Was she talking about Nash or the cows?

"I'll look on this side of the creek and near the east pond. There are plenty of wooded areas where she might have gone to have that calf. I'll search those, too."

"It's raining again. Hard. And it's cold." Monroe reached for her crutches. "Besides, you're in a stew over Nash showing up after all this time.

You aren't thinking straight. You shouldn't go off alone when you're distracted this way."

Harlow was tired of talking. She needed to get back outside, rain or shine, and do some serious thinking. Alone was exactly what she wanted.

"Speaking of stew," she said with a quirk of her lips, "make that for dinner. It'll warm me up when I get back."

Monroe rolled her eyes toward the ceiling. "Stubborn."

"Takes one to know one."

Her sister snorted. "Ain't that the truth?"

All three of the Matheson sisters had a stubborn streak a mile wide.

A door downstairs closed with a bang.

Monroe hobbled to Harlow's side and peered around her shoulder. "Poppy's back."

Harlow frowned. "How did he make such a quick trip to the ER?"

"Maybe Pop dumped you-know-who on the side of the road and spun mud in his face."

Next door, three-year-old Davis cxited his bedroom, toting a plastic fire truck, his dark cowlick aloft on the back of his head. This week he wanted to be a fireman. Last week, he'd been set on becoming a bald eagle.

"Who, Mommy? Who did Poppy dump in the mud?"

"Nobody, baby. Your aunt was joking."

Under her breath so only Harlow could hear, Monroe muttered, “No, I wasn’t.”

Shaking her head, Harlow hurried down the stairs and into the kitchen. She’d have laughed if the situation wasn’t so concerning.

“You’re back already?” Harlow said to her granddad as he plunked his hat on the rack beside the back door.

“Nash insisted I take him to his house.”

“Was he better?”

“Looked to me like he was hurting worse than the nose of a mule-kicked pup. He’s tough, though, tried not to let on.”

Like most professional athletes, Nash had the pain tolerance of a granite boulder. He shrugged off discomfort and kept moving. That he’d displayed his pain in front of them said a great deal about how badly he hurt.

Stifling the inclination to feel sorry for the man, Harlow offered her grandpa a dry kitchen towel.

Poppy wiped off his face before shrugging out of his wet slicker. A puddle formed where he stood. Harlow went to the closet for the mop.

“I figure one of us needs to go over there later and check on the boy,” Poppy said.

Harlow tensed, her fingers tightening around the mop handle.

That *boy* was a grown man. A massive, anvil-bodied male who could take care of himself or call one of his famous friends to come to the rescue. The Mathesons had done all they should ever do for the likes of him.

"Why would we want to do that?"

Poppy narrowed his eyes in mild reproach. Since coming to know Jesus, she was trying to be more Christlike, like her grandpa, but Nash Corbin pushed every anger button inside her.

Poppy slowly draped the tea towel over the back of a chair. "If something happens to him over there alone, how will you feel?"

She rubbed the mop against the floor with more vigor than was required. "He's capable of looking after himself."

"Says the woman who hauled him out of the pasture this afternoon, unconscious."

The mop paused in midscrub.

Why did her grandpa have to be right all the time?

She went back to scrubbing.

Right or wrong, she was not nursing Nash Corbin back to health.

She flicked Poppy a quick glance. "You know how I feel about him. How we *all* should feel."

For more reasons than you know.

Poppy's white eyebrows lifted like the wings of doves. "Neighbors look after neighbors, little girl."

"Really?" Harlow bristled. "The way he looked after us?"

The old man blanched, mustache quivering suspiciously. He slid his eyes to one side and went still as midnight.

Regret stabbed Harlow in the heart.

She shouldn't have said that. They never talked about that awful time, and her grandpa refused to let any of them say an evil thing about Nash Corbin.

But now, she'd opened her big mouth and hurt Poppy's feelings.

Before she could apologize, Poppy, who suddenly looked like the old man he was, quietly left the room.

Harlow squeezed her temples between thumb and forefinger. She wasn't herself today. Thanks to the lost cow, a pressing mortgage payment—two of them—and Nash Corbin's unexpected reappearance, she was on edge to the extreme.

Nonetheless, her stress was no reason to hurt Poppy. He'd believed in Nash and thought he was doing a wonderful thing that would bring prosperity to his family. Her grandfather, with every good intention, had willingly agreed to an investment that had nearly wiped them out financially. Poppy had suffered for it, too, knowing he'd trusted unworthily, aware that his bad decision had jeopardized the futures of every person on the Matheson Ranch.

Yet, after all that, Poppy still believed the best about everyone. Because his own personal code of ethics was strong as a mountain, he expected the same, fair treatment from others.

Sometimes that expectation came back to bite him.

Even now, he'd do the scriptural thing by the man who'd cheated them.

"Do good to those who spitefully misuse you," he'd say.

Harlow's resentment of Nash did not give her the right to say something hurtful to her grandpa. She owed him everything, especially respect.

Guilt riding her shoulders, she leaned the mop against the wall and hollered up the stairs. "Monroe, Davis, I'll be back later."

Monroe appeared at the top of the steps.

"Determined to find that calf?"

"No. I'm trying to apologize to Poppy."

Before Monroe could question the curious statement, Harlow exited the house and headed to the enemy's camp.

Chapter Four

Was he dreaming? Or was someone knocking on the door?

Prying his eyelids up, Nash tried to rise from the couch. He failed.

The *tap-tap-tap* came again.

Great. Just great. His presence had already been discovered.

Hopefully not the press.

Or his agent.

But who else?

He let his eyelids fall.

Maybe if he didn't answer, the visitor would decide he wasn't in the house after all and leave.

"Nash," a familiar female voice called through the door, "are you okay?"

His eyes popped open.

Harlow?

She already knew he was here. He needed to let her in and convince her not to say a word to anyone.

Had he already done that? He couldn't remember.

Using all his remaining strength he called, "Door's unlocked."

He let his eyes fall closed again.

Nash heard Harlow enter, heard the door snick shut behind her. His head hurt too much to look at her.

If there was one person on earth he trusted not to post a social media photo of him lying on a dusty couch, covered by a throw rug, wet and shivering and half dead, it was Harlow. But he had to ask. He had to be sure.

A cold hand touched his forehead.

"You're roasting. Why didn't you go to the ER?" She sounded gruff, scolding him with the same tone his sixth-grade teacher had used when Nash had seen the boys' bathroom flooding and hadn't said a word.

What was Harlow mad at him about? Was it because he hadn't been in contact in so long?

"Can't," he mumbled.

She moved her hand, which had felt really good. Weird, considering how cold he was.

"Can you make it to your bed?"

"No." He probably could, but he didn't want to.

He heard her huff, as if his ailment annoyed her. It sure annoyed him.

He pried one eye open to see Harlow leave the living room. The scant light nearly blinded him.

She returned with a pair of sweats and a stack

of blankets. They probably smelled musty, but he wasn't in any situation to be particular.

She plunked them on the coffee table. "You need to change out of those wet clothes. Can you eat or drink anything?"

"No."

"Can I call anyone for you?"

"No." *But you could stay awhile and act a little friendlier.*

"Fine. I have work to do."

Nash's eyes flew wide open. A rocket launch of pain shot through the top of his head, but he couldn't let her leave just yet. "I need a favor."

She huffed another annoyed breath and perched a hand on her blue-jeaned hip. "What is it?"

"Don't let anyone find out I'm here."

Her nose, that cute little nose of hers, wrinkled in distaste. "You've already made that clear. Several times."

He had? "I can't go into town."

"There you go then. You won't be discovered."

She wasn't making this easy.

Drawing on his remaining reserve, he muttered, "There aren't any supplies in the house. No food. No medicine."

When he'd roared into town, he'd still been too riled up to think of supplies. He just wanted to hide out and think.

Her eyebrows shot up. "Are you asking me to go shopping for you?"

His eyelids wouldn't stay open any longer. "Would you?"

"Of course. Shopping for you would be a privilege." Was that sarcasm he heard in her voice?

Before he could muster up the energy to ask what he'd done, other than getting sick and becoming a nuisance, to upset her to this extreme, the front door opened, then closed with a decided snap, and he was alone again.

By the next morning, the rain had stopped, although Harlow knew the reprieve was temporary. More rain was forecast.

Last night's encounter with an inert, sick Nash and his request that she be at his beck and call like one of his groupies had so enraged her that she'd had a hard time sleeping.

At dawn, she'd risen to push a pencil on the ranch's finances, trying to figure out how to rake up the money for two mortgage payments. Monroe and Poppy knew they were in dire straits, but she refused to worry them with exactly how dire those conditions were. Neither was in any shape to do anything about them.

The responsibility rested on her.

After a worrisome hour of staring at figures that refused to change, it had finally occurred to her to pray. She did, not expecting much. The Lord helped those who helped themselves, didn't He?

Harlow considered her liquid assets. The only

things she personally owned of any value were her horse and her mother's rings.

At one point, she went to her top dresser drawer and took out the small, white jewelry box. Antiques, the engagement ring and wedding band had originally belonged to her mother's grandmother, who'd married into an oil rich family. Though the family wealth was long gone, the diamond and platinum wedding set remained. After her parents' deaths, each of the sisters received a piece of their mother's antique jewelry. Harlow's gift had been the rings. She treasured them, had dreamed of someday wearing the set as a bride just as three generations of women before her had done.

Though it hurt to consider selling, she wondered if Mom's rings were the answer to her prayers.

Stewing, gnawing her bottom lip until it felt raw, she put the rings away and shoved the drawer closed.

Not yet. There had to be another way.

Selling more livestock was out of the question. They'd already sold off as much as they could without giving up the "seed" as Poppy termed the young cows and calves. Any more and there would be no Matheson Ranch.

She couldn't let that happen to Poppy. This ranch was in his blood. Cowboying was all he'd ever known.

Thinking of cowboying, she put away her pen and paper and headed out into the cold, rainy morning to search for the missing cow-calf pair. With daylight breaking, she saddled Burr and took Ollie the collie along. The well-trained cow dog would assist in finding and bringing in the cattle, if they were still alive.

As she rode the pasture, over rises and along the wooded creek, her gaze repeatedly moved northward toward the Corbin Ranch. Another worry she couldn't resolve.

After an hour of searching with drizzle dampening her already damp mood, Ollie disappeared into the underbrush and yipped, a sign that she'd found something.

After a brief tussle, Harlow won the battle to toss the new, still alive but wet, shivering, newborn calf over the saddle knowing the mama would follow her baby to the barn. If the cow balked, Ollie would get her moving.

"Thank you, Lord," she whispered.

Maybe God felt sorry for her, considering she had enough disasters on her hands without adding a dead cow and calf.

Stepping inside the back door of home, the warmth, along with the smell of bacon, welcomed her.

The Matheson house was an older frame farmhouse from another era. Nothing fancy in the least, but the place was homey, cozy and filled with love and the people who mattered. Other than Taylor who, at last text, was somewhere in Montana hiking the mountains with friends. People Harlow didn't know. Taylor knew her propensity for making friends with anyone and everyone drove her big sister up a wall.

"You're just in time." Poppy stood over the stove, dishing up breakfast. He glanced at her over one shoulder. "Feed bag's on. Sit."

Harlow washed up at the sink, poured a mug of coffee, and joined Monroe and Davis at the scarred kitchen table. On special occasions, she covered the old wood with a tablecloth, but mostly, she liked the table as it was. Generations of Mathesons had eaten here, leaving their marks—literally—in the wood.

"Cow and a healthy bull calf are in the barn."

Poppy scooped the final fried egg onto the platter. "Praise the Lord Jesus."

"I already did."

"Never can do it enough." Poppy plunked the platter of food onto the table next to Monroe's biscuits. Monroe wasn't much of a cook, but she baked great biscuits.

They offered grace and ate in silence for a few minutes.

When Poppy had polished off two eggs and several slices of bacon and was in the process of adding strawberry jam to a biscuit, he said,

"I figure you need to look in on the Corbin boy again this morning."

Monroe and Harlow exchanged glances. Harlow didn't say anything even though she was thinking plenty. Poppy knew how she felt. No point in hurting his feelings again.

She was still mulling the unwanted shopping trip.

If Nash felt better, he was probably hungry. If he wasn't better, he still needed sustenance and medicine.

She didn't want to care whether he got well or not, but she did.

Her grandpa must have noticed the instant tension in the room because he looked at Monroe and then at her for several uncomfortable seconds. Quietly, he finished his breakfast and then went for his Bible, as he did every morning.

"Got some interesting reading in today's devotional," he said. "Matthew 5, the Sermon on the Mount. Jesus's best sermon, I'm thinking."

Poppy patted the top of Davis's hand and spent several minutes painting an elaborate word picture for the little boy about Jesus sitting on top of that big old mountain surrounded by folks who'd sit and listen to him all day without a bite to eat.

"Now, that's devotion, Davis. They knew he was giving them more than natural food." Poppy patted the striped shirt pocket that covered his heart. "Food for the soul."

"I like Jesus," the boy said, bringing smiles to the faces of every adult.

"He likes you, too." Monroe wiped a jelly smudge from the corner of the three-year-old's mouth.

"Now," Poppy went on, "on this particular day, Jesus was talking to his disciples, a bunch of rabble-rousing hardheads who had a lot to learn. And He said something important that just about blew their hats in the dirt."

Smoothing a weathered hand lovingly over the thin paper, he read, "'But I say unto you, love your enemies, bless them that curse you, do good to them that hate you, and pray for them which despitefully use you, and persecute you; That ye may be the children of your Father which is in heaven: for He maketh his sun to rise on the evil and on the good, and sendeth rain on the just and on the unjust.'"

He glanced up. "Now, this next part is even more important. 'For if ye love them which love you, what reward have ye? Do not even the publicans the same? And if ye salute your brethren only, what do ye more than others? Do not even the publicans so? Be ye therefore perfect, even as your Father which is in heaven is perfect.'"

Sliding a bookmark into place, he patted the page. "You get that, son? Even if someone does a cowpoke wrong, we got to treat 'em good. That makes us perfect in God's eyes. Now, perfect here don't mean never messing up. It means mature. Grown up. We act like a grown-up because it's what Jesus would do. We do the right thing, the Jesus thing, even if others do us wrong. His way is always right even when we don't like it."

He clapped the Bible shut, rose from the table and limped out of the room.

Davis might not be able to understand, but Harlow certainly got the point. From Monroe's contrite expression, so did she.

Nash had hurt them, done them wrong, caused them many problems, but Jesus commanded that every wounded Matheson rise above their personal feelings and show Christ's compassion and forgiveness.

Which meant a shopping trip for the enemy next door.

The sweet biscuit turned bland on her tongue.

Poppy had always found a way of correcting the three sisters without lifting a hand.

An hour later, Harlow grudgingly roamed the aisles of the IGA store for anything she thought Nash might need. Considering his stomach problem, he could get dehydrated, so she tossed in a pack of Gatorade. Didn't athletes drink that stuff by the tubful?

Soup would be good. Crackers. A few over-the-counter medicines. Mac and cheese for when he felt better. Nash loved mac and cheese. Or once had. He said Poppy made the best mac and cheese in the world, which was hilarious, considering it came from a box.

Back then, the boy next door was at her dinner table as often as he was at home. He'd eat anything and lots of it.

She tossed in a few cans of spaghetti and ravioli. Then she put them back on the shelf. Weren't professional athletes on special diets?

She perched a hand on one hip and glared at the rows of canned goods.

What now?

With a shrug, she reclaimed the cans.

Considering she didn't know what that special diet was and Nash was so worried about his privacy being invaded by his hordes of adoring fans, he'd have to deal with whatever she gave him.

If he didn't like her choices, he'd have to come into town himself. Except he couldn't right now. He was too sick.

And Poppy would be upset if she didn't do her best by the man who'd nearly ruined them.

Mr. I'm So Important That I Have to Hide was giving her an ulcer. Why did he have to come *here* to escape his fame? Why not Antarctica or deep in the Amazon jungle?

After adding a few more of what she considered kitchen staples to the basket, she rolled to the cashier and began unloading the items onto the conveyer belt.

The cashier, Ashley Renner, whom Harlow had known as long as she could remember, wiped her hands on a paper towel and smiled before reaching for the first item to scan. "Hey, Harlow, how's it going?"

"Same old, same old." Boy, was that ever stretching the truth.

"I hear ya. This rain is something, huh?" Ashley swept the milk across the scanner.

"Sure is. Cold, too."

"Jenna Bates was in here earlier. She said Sundown Creek is about to flood over the bridge again. She lives out that way, you know." *Beep. Beep. Beep.* Her hands moved as fast as her mouth. "Sure hope the weather improves before the Strawberry Festival. The whole town will be disappointed if we have to cancel."

Harlow plopped a giant jar of peanut butter onto the counter next to the grape jelly and a loaf of wheat bread. "Especially the kids. My church small group is building a float. So is the youth group."

"My littles are going to be part of a garden float. Gracie's a ladybug and Matthew's a sunflower. The costumes are adorable, but they've about given me an earworm from singing 'The Ants Go Marching One by One.'" Ashley laughed and quickly beeped five cans of soup. "Is Davis riding in the parade this year?"

Harlow frowned, remembering the dilemma

waiting for her in the Corbin Ranch house. "I don't know. He's really little."

"You could ride that beautiful horse of yours and keep Davis in the saddle with you."

"Maybe." Hopefully, Nash would be gone by then, back to his adoring fans and rich life. If she could just keep him away from Davis until that happened.

"Is Preach Beckham still trying to buy him?" Laughing, Ashley fluttered her hands above the scanner. "I mean your horse, not your son."

Harlow laughed too, though she couldn't help wondering if Nash would think he could buy Davis if he discovered the truth. Money was a powerful thing.

"Always. He asks me at least once a month."

"And every time you refuse. Must be some horse."

"Burr is from Yates Trudeau's stock and the best I've ever owned." She knew she sounded defensive, but Ashley had no way of knowing that she'd considered, if only for a second, selling Burr that very day.

Burr had listened to her sobs after Nash had left. He'd listened again when she'd discovered the pregnancy. From strong bloodlines, the golden palomino was an excellent cow horse. She didn't know how she'd work cattle without him.

Thanks to Nash's underhandedness, she and her family had lost a lot. But they still had their ranch, some keepsakes of her mother's and their animals. None of them were for sale.

Nash thought he might live. But he wasn't sure if he wanted to.

He'd awakened the next morning, still weak and feverish, but capable of changing into the sweats Harlow had left on his coffee table. All he'd managed last night was to pull both the blankets over his shivering body. After that, he didn't recall anything until a shaft of sunlight startled him awake.

His head still pounded.

Whatever tried to kill him was a tenacious sucker.

Throat as dry as the Mojave, he was contemplating the long journey to the kitchen when a tap sounded on his door and, before he could call out, Harlow shoved her way inside, a grocery bag in each arm.

She took one glance at him before heading into the adjacent kitchen. So much for friendly greetings.

What was her problem anyway?

She stuck her head around the doorway. "I bought soup and Gatorade. You owe me sixty-two dollars."

For soup and Gatorade? Wow, prices had escalated.

Did he even have sixty-two dollars?

"I didn't know if you'd return."

"I'm here." She disappeared back into the kitchen to bang cans and what have you onto the worn Formica counter.

The noise hurt his head.

Pushing back the pile of musty blankets, he eased to an upright position, feet on the floor, head in hands. His brain made circles inside his skull.

Dizzy, light-headed, weak. Man, he was a mess.

Through his fingers, he saw a bottle of Gatorade appear on the coffee table.

"Thanks." He looked up. A pulse throbbed behind his eyes. Harlow looked a little wavy. He reached for the Gatorade. It looked wavy too.

"I'll heat the soup," she said. "Chicken noodle okay?"

His stomach rolled. "Perfect."

He sipped at the Gatorade until Harlow brought the soup. She perched on the chair opposite the couch, watching his hand shake as he tried to spoon the liquid into his mouth.

There was something in her expression that he didn't understand. Animosity, maybe. Fear? For certain, she was tense as a fiddle string in the key of E, as Gus would say.

But why? He and Harlow, the whole Matheson crew, had been great friends. Was she angry because he hadn't kept in touch?

"It's good to see you, Harlow."

"Why are you here after so long?"

So that was it. She was angry about his long silence. He had to admit, he deserved her anger. He should have called, texted, emailed or something.

"Personal problems," he said.

Her lip curled. "I can only imagine how tough your life must be."

"Everyone has problems, Harlow." He wasn't about to tell her of the mess he'd made of things, but the shoulder injury was common knowledge. "Tore my shoulder up. Had surgery a few days ago."

Harlow's bird-wing eyebrows dipped. "A few days? And you were out last night in that weather? You could have an infection in that arm."

Fear snaked down his back, cold, icy. She was right. An infection could account for the sudden illness. With an infection he could be out of the game for an extended time. He could lose his career. Which meant he might never have the opportunity to regain the fortune his agent had stolen from him

"You should see a doctor, Nash." Was that concern he heard in her voice?

"I can't."

"Why?"

He couldn't tell her.

"I need some time away from everyone, Harlow. Some R and R, peace and quiet. I can't deal with media and people right now."

He gave up on the soup and put the bowl on the coffee table. The spoon clattered against the potteryware. He leaned his head against the back of the couch, exhausted.

Silence ticked in the ranch house. His gaze found Harlow and stayed there awhile. Even in ranching work attire of boots and worn jeans, she was peachy pretty with her red hair in a long, loose sweep over each shoulder.

She caught him looking and rose from her perch on the edge of a fake leather easy chair.

"Should I leave the soup or dump it?" She reached for the bowl.

He caught her wrist. "Leave it."

Funny how he couldn't turn loose of her though he knew he should. Harlow glanced down and back up with a pointed look.

"Are you mad at me, Harlow?" he asked.

"Of course not. I don't even know you anymore."

Ah. There it was again. "I should have kept in touch."

"You always dreamed of leaving this town and making it big. Your dreams came true."

They had. Until they became a nightmare.

"What about you, Harlow?" he asked softly. "Did your dreams come true?"

"I have everything that matters." She pulled her hand from his grasp and looked toward the door as if planning a prison break. “Unless you need something else, I have work to do at home.”

“Will you come back?”

“You can call if you aren’t up to taking care of yourself.”

“I can’t. No phone.”

“You don’t have a cell phone?” Her tone was incredulous.

He shook his head. It punished him by hammering his skull. “Left it behind. I wanted to get away for a while, remember?”

“Oh, that’s right.”

Did she just roll her eyes at him?

“Listen, Harlow, I—” What could he say other than, “I’m sorry. You were my best friend.”

“And you ghosted me.”

“The phone rings both ways. You could have called me.”

“I wasn’t the one who left.” She started toward the door, then turned back. “We’ll keep your secret, Nash, but I’d advise you to move that fancy car if you don’t want anyone to know you’re here.”

The sports car. In his pathetically ill state, he’d completely forgotten about it. “Thanks. I’ll move it to the barn.”

“Give me the keys. I’ll move it.”

“Can you drive a stick?” He shook his head, felt the hammer start up again. “Never mind. I know you can,” he said with a slight smile. “Better than me.”

He retrieved the keys from the jeans he'd dumped on the floor in exchange for the dry sweat pants and held them out. All without rising. He couldn't. He was that weak.

Harlow's face, heretofore made of stone, softened until he thought she might even laugh. "You were a gear grinder."

"You had a need for speed."

The smile bloomed. "Still do."

Finally, he'd broken through her wall and gotten a glimpse of the old Harlow. Four years had made her even prettier. Was she still as sweet and kind?

"Don't be joyriding my 'Vette."

The smile disappeared. She snatched the keys from his outstretched hand. "I don't make promises I can't keep."

She exited the house, leaving him to contemplate the sudden shift in her mood.

Chapter Five

Over the next week, Harlow paid a daily visit to their sick neighbor. At one point, Poppy had offered to "check on the boy," but he'd wanted to take Davis along for the company. After Harlow recovered from a near heart attack at the thought, she'd convinced her grandfather that Nash might be contagious and she didn't want to risk either of them falling ill.

A softy when it came to his grandson, Poppy had relented. Plus he claimed she needed a lesson in loving thy neighbor, another statement that nearly caused apoplexy.

As Nash's health improved, Harlow found it harder and harder to maintain a cool distance. He was charming, witty, handsome to the extreme and a reminder of the dreams she'd once had that he didn't share.

Back then, he'd known all her deepest secrets except one. That she'd wanted to be more than friends with her next-door neighbor. A dream that had died when he'd left and had turned to bitter resentment when he'd never even acknowledged the financial collapse he'd caused.

Poppy had been crushed. Maybe that was the worst of her anger. Seeing her grandpa broken and broke because he'd trusted the wrong man. At eighty years old, after a lifetime of striving and hard work, Poppy shouldn't have to struggle back from the bottom.

Perhaps the daily trek to the Corbin Ranch to "check on the boy" was her penance for all that pent-up animosity.

Anytime that animosity faded, she reminded herself of the loss…and of the little boy Nash had left behind.

When her conscience pecked a little, reminding her that Nash did not know about Davis, she ignored it. His ignorance of the fact was his own fault.

This particular morning, with a chilly, Oklahoma wind stirring the naked-branched trees, the rain had blessedly paused to take a breath. Behind gray clouds, the sun made occasional, if feeble, attempts to exert itself.

Harlow crossed the backyard toward the loafing shed where the farm truck was parked. The soggy ground squished beneath her boots. Cold air snaked beneath her hoodie and prickled the skin on her back.

As she reached the truck and yanked open the door, she spotted a figure jog-walking across the pasture. Jog ten steps. Walk. Walk. Walk. Jog again and then bend over, hands to his knees.

Her heart lurched. Nash? What was he doing out in this weather after being sick for days and days? Was he out of his head again? Delirious? Feverish?

Just as quickly, a more disturbing realization slapped her in the face. Nash was making a beeline toward her back porch.

Slamming the truck door with a metallic bang that echoed over the farm and caused a cow or two to look up hopefully in anticipation of fresh hay, she jogged out to meet him.

He'd stopped, hands on knees again, and was puffing like a steam engine.

"Get in the truck. I'll take you home."

He shook his head. "No."

That was all he could manage for a long minute while Harlow considered dragging him to the pickup.

When he finally regained his breath, he straightened and grinned at her. "I'm better."

"I see that. But as Poppy would say, you'll take a setback. Let's get you in the truck and back to your place. The air's too cold and wet out here."

Hopefully, he'd take the tension in her voice as concern for his well-being.

As if he'd lost his hearing as well as his senses,

and in spite of her excellent suggestion, he commenced walking toward the back of the house.

"Nash. No." She jogged to catch up.

He stopped, waited, a quizzical expression on his face. "Just want to say hello and thanks for looking after me while I was sick."

"Consider us thanked." She grabbed his arm. It was harder than steel. The illness hadn't diminished his well-honed physique. Nor had time diminished her acute awareness of Nash as a man. Not a buddy, but an attractive male she cared about. Still.

And if that didn't upset her applecart, nothing would.

Gritting her teeth against the flash of attraction and the memory of the affection they'd once had for one another, she leaned toward the truck, tugging hard on his arm and going nowhere.

"Seriously," he said, as immovable as an 18-wheeler. "I'm back on my feet, feeling human enough to come for my horse and ride him home."

Still holding his arm in a death grip, Harlow pivoted toward the barn and tugged. "Okay. Great. Drifter is out here."

Two hundred plus pounds of athletic muscle stuck his feet to the ground. Harlow skidded to a stop.

Nash squinted at her. "Are you trying to get rid of me?"

"No!" *Yes*. "I'm concerned about your health. You could run out of energy, pass out again."

He grimaced. "Please don't tell anyone I passed out."

She rolled her eyes. "Macho doesn't cut it with me, bud."

His grin made her want to grin back. "Never did. It was what I liked about you, Harlow. Still do. You're genuine."

She was who she was, including the mother of his son. Would he still think of her as genuine if he knew that? "Unlike your friends down in Florida?"

His grin faded like new blue jeans in hot water.

"Some." He shrugged. "More than I expected. But *you* never had an agenda."

She did now.

Before she could convince him to follow her to the barn where they'd stabled his black horse, Poppy slammed out the back door and limped in their direction. His cane rhythmically punched holes through the wet grass.

"Nash, boy," he hollered, his tone gruffly concerned. "I thought that was you. What are you doing out in this weather? Get in this house before you take a setback and get pneumonia." He pronounced it pee-numonia.

Defeated, Harlow watched with fear and trembling as the big athlete followed her hobbling grandpa into the kitchen.

"Please, Lord," she muttered, "keep Davis upstairs."

Some prayers didn't get answered. Or if they did, the answer was no.

Three-year-old Davis, his brown rooster tail of a cowlick aloft, sat at the kitchen table poking syrupy pancakes in his mouth. He looked up, curious about the unexpected visitor.

"Sit down there, Nash." Poppy motioned to the table. "Coffee's still hot."

With a tired and obviously relieved sigh, Nash eased onto a chair opposite Davis. Naturally, his gaze fell to the little boy.

Harlow's whole body went on red alert.

What would he see when he looked at her son? *His* son?

"Hi," he said. "I'm Nash. What's your name, big guy?"

"Davis." The boy poked another syrupy bite into his mouth.

"You like pancakes?"

Davis nodded, his mouth too full to speak.

Harlow stood frozen near the back door, holding her breath, afraid of what might happen next. So far so good. Nash hadn't tensed or turned on her with a knowing glare. Wasn't he curious about the child who hadn't been here four years ago when he left? Wouldn't he wonder where the boy had come from?

When Poppy set a coffee mug in front of Nash and shot her a questioning glance, she forced herself to move.

Monroe was nowhere in sight, so she had no coconspirator to come to the rescue. She was on her own, praying to dodge the bullets no one in the room knew were flying except her.

"You had breakfast yet, son?" Poppy waved his spatula toward Nash. "Got plenty of pancake batter."

That Poppy could still call the athlete "son" told a great deal about his determination to forgive and forget. She could forgive—maybe—but she'd never forget. She literally couldn't.

"Not sure I can handle them yet, Gus."

"Belly still a tad tetchy?"

Nash grinned in that charming, self-deprecating way of his that made Harlow's heart flutter. Or used to. Any flutter now was pure terror.

"A tad," he agreed. "But those pancakes smell tempting."

"A good sign. I'll fix you one to try, but don't feel obligated."

"Appreciate it, Gus, and all you and Harlow have done for me this past week."

"Neighbors help neighbors."

Right. Like Nash had helped them. Poppy's statement burned fire down her spine. She wanted to spit and holler and throw his double-dealing treachery in his face, not ply him with hot coffee, pancakes and kindness.

As if he was completely unaware of Nash's awful betrayal, Poppy cooked a trio of pancakes and put one filled plate in front of Nash and another in the empty spot next to Davis.

"Sit and eat, little gal," he said to Harlow. To Poppy anyone younger than fifty was still little.

"Aren't you going to eat?" she asked him.

"Done did." He reached for his coat and hat on the peg by the back door. "I've got to move hay this morning before more rain comes in."

No, he didn't. With his bad knees, he was more liability on the ranch than help.

Harlow started to rise. "I can do it."

One of Poppy's mild looks sat her back down. "So can I. You have enough to handle. I'm still capable of driving a tractor."

"I know, Poppy, I just—" Before she could finish the sentence, he snapped the door closed on her protests. "Stubborn old man."

"Like his granddaughter." Nash's tone was light, friendly.

Harlow dragged a chair up to the table and stared at the pair of pancakes she didn't want. She, Nash and their son were alone in the kitchen. If she tried to eat anything, she'd choke to death.

A thousand emotions stampeded through her chest. Fear, anger and, despite everything, affection crept in. Plus regret. Even if he didn't know it, she'd loved this man. He'd given her Davis. But he'd also broken her heart and those of her family. Yet, he was still as hound-pup friendly as ever.

Did he feel no remorse?

She wanted to ask, but was reminded of her promise to Poppy. Say nothing. The Holy Spirit could do more on the inside of a person than all the talking any human might do. Let the Lord work on the man's conscience.

He was sure working on hers.

Using the side of his fork, Nash sliced off a small bite of pancake and nibbled the edges. No butter, no syrup. Proof that his stomach was more than a tad tetchy.

He was not as well as he let on.

Do not feel sorry for him. And stop staring at him!

Harlow cut into her own unwanted breakfast and pushed a forkful around her plate, trying to think of a distracting conversation and coming up blank.

Nash, who could wring conversation from a doorknob, started an easy discussion with Davis about the merits of blueberry vs chocolate chip pancakes.

Her bright penny of a child, warming to this new, interested audience quickly segued to fire trucks and *Veggie Tales*.

"*Veggie Tales*?" Nash asked. "Is that the cartoon with carrots and tomatoes?"

"Uh-huh. And Larry."

"Is he the lasagna? Larry, the lasagna."

This silliness brought giggles from Davis. Shaking his head from side to side, he covered his mouth with a sticky hand.

Nash pretended affront. "What? Don't you like Larry, the lasagna?"

"He's not lasagna. He's a 'cumber."

Nash glanced at Harlow for clarification. "'Cumber?"

"Cucumber," she said, smiling. Not at Nash. At her son's adorable language. Though she had to admit her eyes were on the handsome athlete filling up her kitchen.

"How did I not know that?" He grinned back at her and in spite of her reservations, Harlow started to relax a tiny bit.

Nothing in Nash's demeanor seemed suspicious as he continued to engage Davis—and her—in random and completely innocent discussions. His charm worked on children as well as it did on women and the press. She could understand why he was a darling of corporate sponsors.

If he wondered, even a little, where this sweet-faced boy had come from, he showed no indication of curiosity.

Or was he simply too polite to ask in front of a child?

Would he later waylay her with questions?

And the biggest concern: Was she willing to lie about Davis's parentage and claim another man had fathered the boy?

The idea stirred acid in her stomach. At this rate, she'd have an ulcer soon.

When was this man going back to Florida and leaving her and her family in peace?

Her tumultuous thoughts were diverted by the thump and thud of Monroe's crutches on the wooden floor. She entered the kitchen, casted leg aloft. Glancing from Nash to Davis to Harlow and, accustomed to making snap decisions under pressure, Monroe maneuvered to Davis and kissed him on top of the head.

"Morning, sugar. About finished? *Puppy Friends* is on." She ran a tender, motherly hand over his rooster tail. "Oh, that hair of yours..."

Eyes wide, the boy looked up. "*Puppy Friends*? Yes!"

Davis grabbed his milk and downed it. After a long, grinning *ahhh* that made the adults smile, he said, "I done."

Leaning on one crutch, Monroe held out a hand. Completely forgetting everyone else in the room, Davis clambered out of his chair, and the pair exited the room to watch the boy's beloved cartoon.

Conversation ceased.

Harlow jabbed a fork into an unwanted piece of pancake.

She was alone. With the enemy.

Except he wasn't. But he could still hurt her if he wanted to.

And that scared her to pieces.

He'd been so sweet to Davis.

Nash sipped at his coffee mug.

As he sat the cup carefully back onto the table, he spoke in a low voice. “I didn’t know Monroe had a son.”

The loaded fork froze halfway to Harlow’s mouth.

He thought Davis belonged to Monroe.

Wasn’t that what she’d hoped he would think?

Except she hadn’t anticipated the question.

To buy time, she shoved in the bite and chewed the over syrupy hotcake. An inward battle commenced. Her conscience waged a war, a holy one.

Allowing the lie to stand would be easy. Maintaining that lie could only lead to more questions and eventual disaster.

Roping Monroe into her mess was wrong.

Lying was wrong, too. Didn’t God say in Proverbs that He hated lies? And didn’t the Bible say the devil was the father of all lies?

She wanted nothing to do with the devil, especially when it concerned her baby.

She loved the Lord and her boy—their boy—too much to deny the truth.

Carefully, she put down her fork.

Swallowing past the knot in her throat, she murmured, “Davis isn’t Monroe’s son. He’s mine.”

Chapter Six

Nash's fork clattered onto his plate. His mouth dropped open.

Harlow had a child? When? With who?

He blinked a couple of times to clear away the shock.

It didn't leave.

Harlow. Davis. Mother and son.

Harlow, his buddy and friend, had a child and he hadn't known about it.

A weed of suspicion sprouted. He uprooted it, tossed it aside like so much crabgrass.

He'd telephoned Harlow to be certain she wasn't pregnant. Twice. She'd claimed no aftereffects of that one night they'd both regretted. Afterward, Sterling, his agent, had followed up and concurred. Harlow wasn't pregnant.

According to his agent, she'd even been dating another guy.

The last thought hit him between the eyes.

She'd been dating someone else.

Had the jerk run out on her and left her son without a dad?

He latched on to the thought but didn't ask Harlow for clarification. None of his business.

Still, he wondered. And he was more than a little angry that some guy had mistreated Harlow.

The worrisome suspicion snuck back in.

He hoped it wasn't him.

No, it couldn't be.

Harlow would have told him. He was sure of it. They were best friends. They talked about everything.

Or once had.

He'd let that friendship fade, an action he regretted now that he'd seen her again and been the recipient of her company and nursing care every day for the past week.

He hadn't known he missed her, but he had.

He *liked* Harlow Matheson. She was real and totally unimpressed with his success.

In fact, during those few days of his illness, Harlow had been as stiff as concrete. He figured she hadn't quite forgiven him for ghosting her, as she called his four-year silence. He understood, didn't hold it against her, though he did regret being the cause of her coldness.

Gradually, as they spent time together, Harlow had loosened up. He'd had to work at it, teasing her and making light conversation even when he hadn't really felt well enough to keep his eyes open. But he'd wanted to see her smile, hear her laugh. He'd *needed* her to be his buddy again.

Sometimes she'd catch herself and stop laughing as though ashamed of having a good time in his presence, but each day she became more like the girl he remembered.

Only this girl had matured into an attractive woman.

Very attractive.

He blinked away a thought that had pressed at him all morning. Yes, he'd jogged over to retrieve his horse. But more than that, he'd wanted to see Harlow.

She looked country girl good. Wholesome. Pretty. Real.

There wasn't a fake thing about Harlow Matheson.

There he went again. Woolgathering about his nurse and neighbor.

Must be a remnant of the fever. Had he suffered brain damage?

He cleared his throat. "Davis seems like a sweet kid."

"He is. The best thing in my life."

"Good. I'm glad." There it was again, that urge to ask about the boy's father.

Part of him wanted to know. Another part didn't.

If he was a father, he owed Harlow more than

he could ever repay. Now that his money was gone, he couldn't even help her with finances.

But if some other man was the father, wouldn't it be insulting to Harlow for him to ask?

Hadn't she all but admitted the other guy was Davis's dad?

While he wrestled with the options, Harlow rose from the table and went to the cabinet above the sink in the long eat-in kitchen.

"Would you like a glass of milk or something easier on the stomach?" she asked.

He'd barely touched the strong coffce.

"Milk sounds good. I don't have any at the house." She knew that. She'd brought the groceries, another favor he owed her for.

She poured the milk and returned the carton to the fridge, her back to him.

"In case you're wondering, Davis's father and I were only together for a short time. Things didn't work out. We broke up. He left us. No regrets, though. He may not have wanted me or a family, but he gave me Davis."

Nash didn't know whether to be relieved or furious. He hadn't been the one to break her heart, to leave her with a child to raise alone. But someone definitely had.

Harlow's heart pounded with such force, she wondered if Nash could hear it. As she placed the milk glass in front of him, her hands trembled the slightest bit. Afraid he'd notice, she quickly reclaimed her chair and twisted her fingers together in her lap.

She couldn't believe she was having a civil conversation in her own kitchen with Nash about their son. The son he didn't know about.

She hadn't lied. Everything she'd told him about Davis's father was true. She and Nash had been together a very short time. He'd never wanted her or a family. He'd wanted success and he'd gotten it. And he'd left. All true.

If Nash guessed anything in her statements was amiss, he didn't question them.

"So, you're doing okay? You and your son?"

"We're more than okay. Mathesons survive and thrive no matter what life hits us with."

"Good. Good. I'm glad. I'm sorry about the guy, that he hurt you."

You should be, you jerk. "As I said, Davis is happy and healthy and I'm fine. That's all that matters now."

Nash picked up the milk glass, stared at the white liquid but didn't drink. "Gus wasn't using a cane when I left for the NFL. What's wrong? Are his knees giving him trouble?"

Poppy's knees. Safe ground. She stopped strangling her fingers, forced her shoulders to relax. "They're worn out, and it infuriates him. Even at eighty he thinks he should be able to do everything he did at forty."

Absently running his thumb back and forth on the moist glass, Nash frowned. "Does he need surgery?"

Harlow forced an easiness she didn't feel into her tone and offered a mental prayer of thanks that the subject had moved to something other than Davis.

"Yes, but he refuses." She drawled the next words in imitation of her grandpa. "No one's cuttin' on him. If the good Lord don't fix him, he'll stay broke."

She didn't mention the fact that Poppy couldn't afford the medical bills and refused to shackle the family with additional debt.

Nash chuckled softly, a warm, friendly, affectionate sound. It seemed out of place on a man who'd ignored her for so long.

"That sounds like Gus. What about Monroe? She was in the navy when I left. Was she wounded?"

"She mustered out after a fire aboard ship." Thinking about the heartache and suffering her sister had endured made her own problems seem small. "She's been through a lot in the last couple of years. Please don't mention the scars to her. She's very self-conscious about them."

"I wouldn't."

He wouldn't have in the past. That he was still the same thoughtful guy messed with her head. How could he show compassion about Monroe's scars, and yet care so little about the disaster he'd caused? Was he too embarrassed to bring it up? Too ashamed?

Yet, he was rich. She'd heard about his multimillion-dollar contract last year. Everyone in Sundown Valley had talked about it for days. If he really cared and if he had a conscience, he could repay them every penny they'd lost.

While her brain stuck on the financial loss like Poppy's old-time records that played the same song over and over driving everyone to distraction, Nash went right on being too friendly.

"Is the leg injury military related too?" He placed the milk on the table, his enormous fingers covering half the glass.

She couldn't help but stare at his hands, hands she'd always admired. They were beautiful in a manly kind of way, the tops smoothly tan and threaded with thick veins and sinew. A narrow, nearly invisible scar ran between the thumb and index finger, courtesy of a hay hook years ago, adding to his rugged appeal.

She'd heard football commentators call them soft hands because of his uncanny ability to vacuum a torpedoing football out of the air, but there was nothing else remotely soft about Nash Corbin.

He'd always had the longest, strongest fingers of anyone she knew. Hands that could once also wrangle a rowdy steer, tenderly pat her back or smooth her hair when she cried.

She missed those hands.

Why had he tossed their friendship away? Was he so ashamed of that one final night together that he'd decided not to think about her at all?

The hurt pushed in, stirring good memories and bad.

She couldn't let it affect her again.

Dragging her eyes away from Nash's hands, she latched on to his question about Monroe.

A little spot in her heart continued to grieve the loss.

"Remember that old shed out behind the barn where we store junk?"

"Sure. I helped you and Gus drag all kinds of useless farm equipment and a broken appliance or two out there."

That's right. He had. Back then, he'd been willing to help around the farm. Poppy claimed it was because he was an only child and he needed the company of other kids.

"Poppy always thought he'd figure out a way to fix that stuff." She smiled, affection for her grandad pushing out more of her tension. "That's Poppy. A born fixer."

Except he hadn't been able to fix her broken heart or the financial disaster Nash Corbin had brought on the family.

"So." Nash patted the tabletop twice, dragging her gaze back to his beautiful, powerful hands.

"What does the shed have to do with Monroe's broken leg?"

She forced her eyes up to meet his. What she saw was the boy she'd known before, not the ogre he'd become in her mind, and that confused her.

"The shed floor rotted. She fell through. Compound fracture. Surgery, pins, the whole enchilada."

"Ouch." He grimaced. "I feel her pain."

"I guess you do. How's your shoulder?"

A troubled expression drew his dark eyebrows downward. He touched a spot along his right shoulder. "Not rehabbing as quickly I'd like."

Harlow reached for her coffee mug, thankful her fingers no longer shook. She'd skillfully diverted his attention away from Davis's parentage. Hopefully, his curiosity was satisfied and the subject was closed. They could share a conversation now and then while he was here, even joke and laugh together about some silly thing they both remembered. All the while, she'd keep praying for him to leave sooner rather than later. Leave her and her son in peace, as he'd done for the past four years.

If the lost money pressed at the back of her brain and her tongue, she had to keep silent or disappoint her grandpa. She'd disappointed him plenty in the past.

"The stomach virus, or whatever it was, must

have set back your shoulder's healing time," she said, impressed by how neighborly she sounded.

"Yeah. Yeah. Probably."

She could see he was concerned about the slow progress. The boy with the big dreams would be devastated to lose that dream now that he'd achieved it. In spite of everything, Harlow felt bad for him.

Talk about conflicted! Her feelings vacillated from loathing to pity to old-time buddies so fast she could suffer whiplash.

"Didn't you say it's only been a couple of weeks since the surgery?" she asked. "Give yourself some time. Now that your belly's better, you can focus on rehabbing the shoulder."

"Yeah." His scowling forehead slowly smoothed. "Thanks, pal."

Before she realized what he was about, Nash stretched a big, beautiful hand across the table and squeezed her fingers. Her hand disappeared beneath his.

She'd always loved when he'd grab her small hand in his giant one to pull her along on some adventure. She'd gone happily, willingly, wherever he led, confident Nash would take care of her.

She'd learned the hard way to take care of herself.

"You always knew how to make me feel better. Don't know what I would have done without you this past week." He squeezed again, gently, his strength leashed, but present. Even after a bout of illness, he was a powerful man. "I've missed you, Harlow."

Heat burned up her neck and over her face. She swallowed hard, trying to hide the emotion banging around in her chest, a difficult task for a redhead.

He'd missed her.

Her heart squeezed harder than the pressure of his hand on hers.

She'd missed him too. So much. So terribly, terribly much.

No. No. No. Not a good idea.

Maybe she'd contracted his illness. She had to be delirious to think like this. Nash had devastated her family. He was the enemy.

Except he was also Nash. The only man she'd ever loved.

Until he'd turned that love to loathing.

She had *not* missed him. She would *not* allow such thoughts to enter her head. She wanted him to go away and never, ever return.

Didn't she?

Fighting the avalanche of confusion, Harlow slid her hand from beneath his, quickly rose and carried her plate to the sink. Behind her, Nash's chair scraped. Metal clinked against pottery as he joined her with his dishes.

If he thought anything odd about her quick departure, he said nothing.

They stood side by side. Like old times. After his comment about missing her, Harlow half expected him to say, "Let's run away. See the world. Ride elephants and climb Mount Everest."

She'd respond with something equally as impossible. "Swim the English Channel. Build an igloo in Antarctica."

Escaping Sundown Valley had been their running joke, especially when he and his dad were at odds over ranch work.

Except he'd done it and she hadn't.

He bumped her side with his. "You never replaced the dishwasher?"

The old machine was one of the appliances he'd helped drag to the shed.

She shrugged. "Dishes are easy to wash. There are plenty of us to do it without needing a machine. As Poppy says, manual labor is good for body and soul."

The excuse sounded good to her. In actuality, they hadn't had the money to replace it after the mess Poppy and Nash had made of their finances.

"Fair enough. You wash, I'll dry?" One dark eyebrow lifted, his shiny brown eyes alight with warmth and friendliness.

Yes, like old times. Except too much muddy water had flowed under the bridge between then and now. Nash may think they could go back to the way things were before, but Harlow knew they couldn't.

"Dish towels still in this drawer?" He put his hand on the outdated drawer pull.

Water sputtered from the faucet as she turned the taps to fill the sink. "Yes. Plenty of things around here have changed, Nash, but not that."

"I hope none of the good things." He pulled a towel from the drawer, bumped it closed with his hip and reached for the first clean dish.

Stop being so nice, she wanted to yell. *Just stop and go away. My head is so messed up now, I'm dizzy enough to fall down.*

And falling was the last thing she could afford to do.

Getting her heart stomped four years ago was a lesson she couldn't, shouldn't, forget.

The water pressure faded to a trickle. She turned the taps off, waited a few seconds, then turned them back on. The water sputtered, coughed, then seemed to find its footing and poured full force from the faucet.

"What's up with the water?"

"Cranky old pipes, I suspect." She scratched her nose with one shoulder. "I hope it's nothing serious."

She handed him a shiny white plate. He swirled the towel over it.

"With Gus's bad knees and Monroe on crutches, looks like you're carrying most of the workload these days."

"I can handle it."

"Give me another day or two to shake this bug, and I can help out while I am here."

Stop being nice.

"You have a bum shoulder." That wasn't the only reason, but the excuse should work.

It didn't. "I have to rehab anyway. This is my second surgery on this shoulder. Remember the one in college?"

"Of course, I do. I helped you get back in shape." As soon as she spoke, she wanted to bite her tongue off. Waxing nostalgic, pretending nothing had changed between them was a fool's game. She would not be his fool ever again.

"Right. You did. So, we both know what I can do and can't during rehab." He winked. "I still have one good arm to hold you with, darlin'."

At the reference to a Sam Elliott line from Poppy's favorite old western, Harlow laughed in spite of herself. He was teasing. The phrase was not a reference to romance.

"Poppy watched that movie again three nights ago. He even has Davis quoting Doc Holliday lines. 'I'll be your Huckleberry.'"

Nash backed away, expression surprised. "You don't let a toddler watch that, do you?"

"Of course not! But Poppy quotes the lines often and Davis mimics anything his grandpa does or says. He's wild about his Poppy."

"Your boy is fortunate to have a good man like Gus as a role model."

"Can't argue that."

She offered him another plate and he caught her eyes. "I'm sorry about Davis's father, Harlow. You deserved better."

Her hand froze on the plate, her gaze locked on Nash's sincere brown eyes.

Two minutes of civil conversation, certain she'd circumvented any more talk of her son's parentage, and herc it was again.

Nash really needed to go back to Florida.

Before she could formulate a sensible reply, her cell phone jangled in her back pocket.

Jerking away from Nash and the truth she hid from him, Harlow dried her hands on the side of her jeans and extracted the ringing phone.

It was Poppy.

"Sis." His voice sounded strained and frighteningly breathless. "I need you to come out here. We got trouble."

Chapter Seven

"Poppy. What's wrong? Poppy!"

Nash saw the worry on Harlow's face as she looked down at the phone and then at him.

Eyes wide, she said, "He hung up."

There was enough fear in those hazel depths to shoot a bolus of pain-relieving adrenaline into his bloodstream. The hair on his scalp actually tingled.

"Does he need help?"

"I think so. He didn't say for certain." She shoved the cell phone into her back pocket. "I don't know what's happened, but he told me to come out there. Now."

Nash tossed the damp dish towel onto the butcher block counter and reached for his jacket. Gus wasn't an alarmist. Just the opposite. If he called for help, something serious was wrong.

From his years of growing up on a farm-ranch, Nash knew that agriculture was one of the most dangerous occupations on earth. Accidents happened. Big animals and bigger machinery increased the risks. Sometimes a rancher got too comfortable with those risks, let down his guard, and tragedy struck.

Gus was a crippled old man with too much stubborn pride to admit when he could no longer do something.

Nash swallowed against a suddenly dry mouth. "Where is he?"

"One of the hay meadows. He didn't say which one." She shrugged into her own jacket and flipped up the hood. "Probably the one closest to the house."

"Let's go."

For once she didn't argue that he was too sick to help. Maybe he was, but he was going out there anyway.

Harlow bolted through the door and ran toward the loafing shed where the flatbed farm truck was parked.

By the time Nash slammed inside the vehicle, his breath wheezed harsh and fast. His knees even shook a little. Rotten virus. After the morning jog and now this mad dash to the truck, he was wearing down fast.

Before he could find his seat belt, Harlow yanked the gearshift into four-wheel drive and barreled across the muddy pasture. Tires spun on the slick earth. The engine whined, bore down, grabbed purchase and jumped forward.

"I hope we don't get stuck," he said.

Harlow shoved the gas pedal to the floor.

Nash pitched toward the dashboard. Each bump jarred his shoulder, shot pain up the side of his neck.

The old truck bounced up and down on the uneven terrain, spinning, growling. Mud splattered and pinged against the undercarriage.

Harlow drove like he remembered. Fast. Hard. Focused.

She was scared. And that shook him. Harlow did not scare easily.

She was, however, a tigress about her family. Understandable after losing her parents in a car accident.

"Horses would have worked better," she muttered, "but I didn't want to take time to saddle up. Poppy didn't sound good. Kind of breathless and faint. I'm afraid he's hurt. If he is, I'd need the truck anyway."

She gnawed her bottom lip, hands tense on the wheel as she leaned forward, scanning the distance for signs of her grandpa.

"Hey." Nash tapped her elbow. "Don't borrow trouble. Maybe he's found a sick cow and can't get her up. Or maybe it's a pack of coyotes."

For her sake, and Gus's, he prayed he was right.

Funny that he'd prayed more since his arrival at the ranch than he'd prayed in the past four years.

Not funny really. Kind of sad. Mom would be disappointed.

But wondering if you were dying coupled with a bad dose of depression from sustaining an injury and going broke all within the space of a week could scare a man into praying.

"I hope you're right." Teeth tight, she glanced his way. "You don't look so good yourself."

He wasn't feeling too great either. Besides the pain in his shoulder, which shouldn't be there, he felt as weak as damp tissue paper.

"I'm all right. Out of shape." He tried for diverting humor.

A man had his pride, and his included not fainting in front of a pretty woman. Even if that woman was once his best friend. Or maybe especially because the woman was Harlow.

An odd consideration, but there it was. He'd missed Harlow a lot more than he'd realized.

"You run fast...for a girl. Got me chugging like a freight train."

Harlow smirked, apparently appreciating his attempt to ease her anxiety. "For a girl" had been another joke between them back in the day. Even with his superior size and speed, she'd had the endurance of a mule and managed to keep up with him.

There was nothing wimpy about Harlow Matheson.

He grinned at her. She grinned back.

Good memories seemed to leap between them. They flooded his thoughts.

The time they'd gotten lost together in the woods while searching for blackberries. They'd been nine. Harlow had gripped his hand, claiming not to be scared because she was with him. He'd felt ten feet tall that day when he'd guided them safely out of the woods.

In high school, she'd stayed up half the night to help him study for a science final. He'd needed that A, and he'd gotten it.

Before he could reminisce out loud, Harlow jerked her gaze away. Most every time they got into a friendly conversation, she'd shift away like this, as if she couldn't stand to remember. She would appear to be enjoying herself and then suddenly freeze like a Popsicle. This time, however, he understood, at least in part. Worry for her gramps crowded out everything else.

Again, she leaned toward the windshield in search of Gus, muttering through clenched teeth, "Where are you, Poppy?"

"Does he still drive that big orange tractor?"

"Yes."

Though the tractor was old, like its owner, it must still be a workhorse. Again, like its owner.

The orange color would help their search.

Slogging along a worn path, leaving deep, muddy ruts someone would have to smooth when the weather cleared, they passed a long row of giant round hay bales.

No sign of Gus.

"He hasn't started moving these yet." She squinted to the left. "He must have started on the back side of the south meadow."

Without slowing down, she whipped the steering wheel toward the south. Nash grabbed the dashboard again and grinned at her need for speed.

"Why is he moving the round bales? They're okay left out in the rain." The square bales required a barn, but not the round ones.

"He wants them closer to the house. Easier for us to feed on really cold days."

Right. He remembered that, though his own dad left the big bales wherever they landed. Mostly, though, Dad had square-baled, and he and Nash hauled that hay to the barn during the hottest part of summer and stacked it high in the stifling tin building. Come winter, Nash had been the one loading hay on the truck again, by hand, this time in the bone-chilling cold, sleet and high winds to feed the cattle.

Jobs he'd vowed never to do again.

Maybe he should sell the ranch along with his Corvette and boat. At least he'd have plenty of money to live on for a while.

Thinking of his own problems depressed him, so he trained his eyes on the open fields in search of an orange tractor.

"There," he said, pointing. "Is that it?"

Harlow jerked the wheel in the direction he indicated and pressed the gas pedal. Tires spun. Mud splatted against the doors and shot big brown blobs onto the windshield. The sturdy Dodge found purchase and lurched ahead.

As they drew closer, Nash's stomach, already a "tad tetchy," tumbled to his running shoes.

Harlow gasped, her peachy skin bleaching pale. "Oh no. Nash. He's rolled the tractor. Oh, Lord Jesus. Please. My Poppy."

Fear snaked up Nash's back. Inwardly, he repeated Harlow's disjointed prayer.

A tractor rollover was one of the most common and deadliest of farm accidents.

And Gus was an old man with bad knees. He didn't move fast anymore. If he hadn't jumped clear of the tractor, he could be under it. Getting crushed by three thousand pounds of farm equipment meant a disaster neither he nor Harlow wanted to consider.

Nash put a reassuring hand on Harlow's arm. Her muscle was tight with tension. "Don't panic. He was able to use his phone. That means something."

Still pale and without looking at him, her head bobbed once.

She was scared to pieces, and Nash wanted desperately to comfort her.

The truck jerked to a halt next to the overturned tractor. Harlow bolted out of the vehicle and raced across the soggy earth before Nash could maneuver his door with one hand. His bad shoulder still didn't cooperate very well, and he was growing more fatigued by the minute.

Dratted virus on top of the surgery had left him short on energy and weaker than a newborn mouse.

Not that he'd let on to Harlow. She'd already seen him at a painfully embarrassing low.

By the time he reached her side, she was on her knees beside Gus, cradling her grandpa's head. The older man was a good two feet from the overturned tractor, though his squashed hat and one boot protruded from under the heavy machine.

Relief flooded Nash like the recent rains.

Gus hadn't been crushed. He'd either been thrown clear or the tractor had caught only one foot and Gus had wiggled out of the boot to crawl away.

Nash closed his eyes and said a quiet prayer of thanks.

Another prayer.

He hoped God would listen after his long silence.

"Poppy." Harlow patted her grandfather's cheek. "Talk to me, Pop. Can you hear me?"

The old man's eyelids fluttered up. "Just resting my peepers."

A ghost of a grin twitched Harlow's mouth.

She flashed a glance toward Nash and back to Gus. He read the worry lingering behind her eyes. They weren't out of the woods. Gus was alive, but his skin was the color of ashes and he lay abnormally still. A well Gus would be blustering and trying to get on his feet.

"Where are you hurt, Poppy?"

"Back's boogered up a tad. Shoulder's smarting some. Elbow feels out of socket." He tried to move his right arm but grunted in pain and stopped. "Watch the elbow, and help me up. The legs are not cooperating."

Nash went to one knee on the soggy ground beside the rancher. Cold moisture seeped through his jogging sweats. He resisted a shiver. "Don't move, Gus. We'll call an ambulance."

Harlow swung her attention from Poppy to Nash. She couldn't believe her ears. Mr. Don't Tell Anyone I'm Here wanted to call an ambulance? If they did, the whole town would be aware of the athlete's presence inside an hour. Was he willing to take the risk? After all his protests about privacy, why would he?

Sincere brown eyes met her shocked stare. "Moving him without medical aid could injure something worse. Better keep him still. You got a blanket in your truck?"

Reasonable. Sensible. But his concern was hard to reconcile.

One minute he was a self-absorbed big shot athlete and the next he was the nice boy next door.

"No blanket." She usually carried one this time of year, but she'd wrapped a calf in it a few days ago. With too much Nash on her mind, she'd forgotten to replace it.

"We need to cover him." Nash began shrugging out of his jacket. "Keep him warm 'til help arrives."

Okay, that was really sweet, the kind of thing Nash of old would do.

A piece of ice chipped loose from her heart and melted all the way down to the toes of her muddy Justin Ropers.

"You'll be sicker. I'll cover him with mine."

Nash ignored her as he carefully slid the sleeve from his injured shoulder.

Poppy clutched Nash's ankle. "Keep your coat, boy. I'm getting up. Got my breath knocked out. That's all."

"You need to be checked over, Gus," Nash insisted, "and make sure nothing worse is going on."

Poppy squinted one eye. "So did you."

"And both of you too stubborn to go." She glared at Nash. "Put that jacket back on!"

He draped it around Poppy's shoulders instead.

"You two arguing is like trying to nail jelly to a tree," Poppy muttered. "No one gains a smidgeon. Now, get me up before my hindside freezes to the mud and we all catch epizooti."

"Poppy," Harlow started.

She loved him too much to lose him. Didn't he understand that? And she was scared. Scared he was more injured than his stubbornness would let him reveal.

"Did the fall knock you out? Were you unconscious?"

Her grandpa flashed a scowl at her. Without replying, which was an answer in itself, he demanded, "Up, I said."

When he used that tone, Poppy meant business.

Harlow shook her head. Stubborn old man.

But her grandfather's mind was stronger than his body. He had every right to make his own decisions. Even when she disagreed.

"Are you able to help me?" she asked Nash.

With an insulted glare, Nash crouched behind Gus, his healthy left arm levering against the older man's back as he used his superior-sized body to gently guide Gus to his feet.

Even though Harlow was concerned about Nash's pallor, she let it go to focus on keeping Poppy upright. Nash was young, healthy and strong. He'd recover. Poppy was old and getting frailer by the day, his once powerful body betraying him. Right this minute, she was certain he was hurt worse than he let on. Wobbly, clearly in pain. Short of breath.

She gnawed her bottom lip, fretting.

Had the tractor injured his chest? Cracked a rib?

Was he having a heart attack?

A scarier thought hit her. Had he had a stroke? Was that why he'd rolled the tractor?

"I'll carry him."

Her gaze snapped to the sickly athlete.

"No, you can't." If he was fit, yes, he could probably run a hundred-yard dash carrying her grandpa. "Your shoulder. And you're still not over the stomach thing."

Poppy, clinging to Nash like a lifeline, straightened as much as he could and fluffed up like a mad rooster. "Nobody's carrying me anywhere."

Pushing away from their support, her grandpa took two steps before he started to go down.

Right before he crumpled onto the mud, Nash slid one broad shoulder against Poppy's chest and hoisted him over his back like a sack of feed.

Poppy grunted once but didn't protest.

Harlow sucked in a gust of cold air, worried about them both.

And Nash toted her grandpa to the truck.

Chapter Eight

Nash required two long, exhausted days to recover from the exertion and the chill he'd taken trying to play the hero. After he'd carried Gus into the house and fussed over him until the older man had run him off, Harlow had driven him back to his ranch. He'd been shivering so hard he'd barely made it into the house. Déjà vu all over again. He spent both days huddled under a blanket sipping hot soup.

His busy, exciting life had deteriorated to deciding what he could eat or taking long naps. How far the mighty had fallen.

Of course, he didn't tell Harlow that carrying Gus twice had nearly wiped him out. She'd have scolded him for doing it in the first place.

But what else could a man do for any injured friend? He'd do it again in a heartbeat, even if he had to use his injured shoulder and every last bit of energy he possessed. Which, come to think of it, he had, at least the energy portion.

Thankfully, Gus wasn't nearly as heavy as the men Nash went up against in games. Or the blocking dummies he practiced on.

With every passing hour and every lazy nap, Nash's strength returned. The old rancher would need a lot more than Nash's few days to recover from *his* injuries.

According to Harlow, Gus still refused to see a doctor, claiming he was only, "stove up." Yet, his back and hip kept him in his recliner most of the time. His ankle had swelled like a balloon. And he wore a makeshift sling on his arm.

Harlow, who studied animal care on the internet, knew a lot about injuries. People medicine, she claimed, wasn't that different from animal care. At least when it came to broken bones or pulled muscles, of which she proclaimed Gus to have the latter. Lots of them to go along with a sprained elbow, a twisted ankle and an abundance of bruises.

By week's end, Nash had shaken the stomach bug and was mostly recovered from playing macho man-toter. Other than the slow-healing shoulder, he felt a good 90 percent.

This morning he'd awakened with a roaring appetite, the first in a while. He wouldn't be surprised if he'd lost a few pounds lately, weight he needed to regain. Getting back in prime playing condition now meant more than rehabbing the shoulder. A scrawny football player wouldn't last long against the big boys.

A fuzzy polka-dot blanket around his shoulders, Nash padded in sock feet into the kitchen. The cupboard wasn't well stocked, but, thanks to Harlow's trips to the grocery store, he had the basics and could fix his own breakfast.

Today, he wouldn't wait around for his neighboring nurse to drop by, although he hoped she would. With no TV reception, no internet and no cell phone, a man could go a little stir-crazy out here alone. He wondered if news of his disappearance was splashed all over social media or if he'd already become a has-been.

His stomach knotted at the thought of losing his job in addition to losing all his money. Right now, he couldn't do a thing about either, so he replaced the thoughts with better ones. Harlow. Her handsome little boy who'd cried when he'd seen Gus in pain.

Sweet child. Polite and friendly, though his three-year-old speech sometimes proved too much for Nash. Harlow was doing a good job with the little guy.

She'd come to his ranch twice the day after Gus's accident and again each day to be sure he hadn't made himself sicker.

She'd scolded and scowled and threatened to post his picture on social media if he didn't take better care of himself. He'd promised to behave, a declaration that had made her snort.

Though spring had to be right around the corner, the old kitchen remained cold. It had always been that way, never warming up until the May heat attacked like a fire torch. And then it had been too hot.

A big change from his deluxe condo in Florida.

He snicked on a couple of burners, filled the coffee maker and turned it on, his mind wandering back to Harlow.

He liked making Harlow laugh. He liked her company.

He liked her. Always had. No change there.

Still, his red-haired neighbor had enough to do with everyone in her household on injured reserve except her. She no longer needed to fuss over him.

Although, he thought, as he opened the fridge, he enjoyed her fussing.

Kind of reminded him of his mama's care. But in a different way that was causing him some concern. Harlow had always been cute. Nowadays, she was way more than a cute, friendly neighbor who had joined him in hiking, riding and fishing. More than the pretty teenager he'd accompanied to her senior prom because Gus had trusted him to keep her safe.

Today, Harlow was an attractive woman.

He didn't know why that bothered him.

He liked that she brought him Monroe's biscuits and sausage or a giant bowl of beef stew. And cookies. Normally he stuck to a healthy diet that excluded rich, buttery cookies, but he ate the ones Harlow baked. Relished them.

Relished her company.

Troublesome.

He frowned at the coffeepot. Coffee still dripped with turtle speed into the throwback carafe, but he snuck a cup anyway while he leaned against the counters and pondered his pretty neighbor.

Sometimes she was edgy as if she didn't like him anymore, and he figured she was still upset about his long silence.

Having learned the hard way that real friends like the Mathesons were hard to come by, he wanted to kick himself for not maintaining their friendship.

He was trying to remedy that failing. If he could ever get healthy. And if Harlow would let him.

Crossing to the sink, he leaned in to gaze out the window. Birds flitted in and out of the red oak where Dad had hung a tire swing for him to play in. He and Harlow had spent hours spinning each other in that thing.

He smiled at the memory.

A pickup truck puttered past on the road adjacent to the ranch. They couldn't see him from this distance, but he moved away from the window anyway.

Amazingly, no one had discovered his whereabouts. The Mathesons, even hard-eyed Monroe who glared at him as if she'd like to skin him alive, had kept their word. He owed them. Especially Harlow.

There she was again.

Some guy out there was missing out on a very fine woman and son. Nash wanted to pry, ask her about the jerk. He would. Eventually. After she'd forgiven him for his long absence. When they were fully comfortable with each other again and could talk about everything.

Maybe then he'd share the disaster he'd made of his life.

Except he was too embarrassed to let her know that a man with a business degree had ignored his own business and lost everything.

She'd always told him how smart he was.

Wasn't that a laugh?

He sipped his coffee and then set the mug aside, knocked the dust off the toaster to cook a couple slices of bread and wished for a pound of bacon. He settled for four eggs and a pint of milk, adding a peanut butter sandwich for dessert.

Protein. Healing required protein.

While he ate, his head clear now that the fever and chills were gone, he sorted through the mess he'd left behind in Florida. His life, his career, his financial future were in serious jeopardy.

He needed to go back, figure things out, contact an attorney. But who? The only attorney he'd ever used was one recommended by his agent, a man he no longer trusted.

He supposed he could ask one of his close teammates for recommendations, but he hesitated to involve them. He didn't even want Zack Rogers, his closest friend and roommate on road trips, to know what an idiot he'd been.

Pondering, he considered that there could be a reasonable explanation for the missing funds.

Should he talk to Sterling Dorsey and give him a chance to explain?

Instantly, he dismissed the thought.

Funds didn't disappear by accident. Someone made them disappear, and it sure hadn't been Nash. The only other person with access to his money was Sterling Dorsey.

A conversation would alert the agent that Nash was on to him, that he knew his portfolio had suddenly disappeared along with his savings and most of his bank accounts. Smart and crafty, Sterling would cover his tracks and run before Nash could do anything to recover his money.

He chomped a giant bite of peanut butter sandwich and worried the situation round and round inside his head, ending right back where he started.

Basically broke, mentally and physically wrecked, and unsure of direction.

Mama would say to pray about it, but he figured his long silence with God didn't give him any right to ask for help. He hadn't asked God's opinion before getting into the mess. Why would God help him get out of it?

His thoughts drifted back to Harlow. Long resistant to her grandfather's faith, she'd become a Christian in recent years. She'd shared that news over a rowdy board game of Sorry, and they'd talked a little about their faith. He'd admitted that he'd lost touch with God in recent years. She hadn't been surprised, a statement that pinched his conscience.

His old friend didn't think too highly of him anymore.

She used to. Had he ruined that friendship with his silence? Or destroyed it the night he'd let things between them get out of control?

His spiritual life. Old friendships. His finances. A lot more than his physical body needed rehabbing.

Holding a garden hose in one hand, Harlow used the other to open the outside faucet next to the barn that fed into the horse troughs. More air sputtered out than water.

With a sigh, she closed the spigot and then tried again.

A weak trickle, followed by more sputters of air, splashed into the trough. The water woes worsened by the day.

"Not a good sign, Ollie," she said to the collie at her side.

The dog's head tilted in question, ears perked toward the hose, as if in agreement.

Water pressure in the house this morning had been the same weak sputter. Weaker even than yesterday and the days before.

She blew out a weary breath and dug her cell phone out of her jacket pocket to look up the phone number of a well service.

Harlow could do many handy-girl chores on the ranch, but she didn't know how to repair an aging water well.

The call connected. She spoke briefly with the business person and asked the price of a service call. The man's reply sent shock waves down her spine.

Reluctantly, she ended the call without making an appointment.

A service call alone was more than she could afford. And that didn't include any actual parts or repairs that might be needed.

They had to have water. She couldn't ask Poppy or Monroe. Neither had that kind of money.

With a heavy heart, Harlow knew what she had to do.

With Ollie at her heel, and fighting against despair, she redirected her energies to finishing the morning's chores. All the while, she desperately sought another solution.

Burr and the other four horses, including Nash's black, Drifter, raised interested heads and plodded in her direction. Nash still hadn't taken him home. Hadn't felt up to it.

The knucklehead had made himself sick again the day of Poppy's accident, though he tried to hide how bad he'd felt when she'd seen him later.

She wrestled a square bale of hay from a stack in the barn and carried it to the corral feeder. Her back complained, but she had enough other problems to deal with. She ignored this one.

Though the morning remained chilled and the air heavy with moisture from the recent rains, the sky had cleared and an encouraging sun warmed her back and shone on the healthy coats of her animals.

Even with the problems heavy on her day, this land, these animals, the connection to God through nature, had a way of bringing her a sense of peace.

Burr nudged his golden nose against Harlow in greeting. Shedding her gloves, she smoothed a hand over his muzzle, never tiring of the velvety feel and his warm, moist breath against her skin.

The patient horse allowed her the privilege of petting him before blowing out a breath and joining the others at the hay. Ollie plopped down to watch, aware her job did not include herding horses.

In the nearest pasture, slick, well-cared-for cattle fed from the giant hay bale she'd put out earlier. Baby calves nursed while their mamas ate breakfast.

These were blessings. She was careful not to forget that. Her life was good even though trouble never seemed to ease off.

Far from the house, the tractor still lay on its side. For the past few days, she'd been too busy taking care of the ranch and the sick and injured to deal with the overturned machine. Eventually, she'd have to ask one of the neighbors to help set it right. Sundown Ranch wasn't far away, and the three Trudeau men were good friends. They'd come if she called.

Just as with the finances, Poppy and Monroe couldn't help moving a downed tractor. The best Monroe could do was hobble around the house and cater to Pop and Davis while Harlow handled the ranch work.

After Nash had set himself back health-wise to rush to her grandpa's aid, she'd stopped resenting the trips to his ranch. This did not, however, change the deeper reasons to resent him. He'd done what he'd done and nothing could erase that, no matter how much Poppy preached forgiveness.

The very fact that the big galoot was only half a mile distant, just across the field, hammered away at her. Fretted her. Intrigued her. Made her remember things best forgotten.

Except she could never forget that they had a

child together. Nash didn't seem suspicious, but, for Harlow, remaining casual when he and Davis were in the same room was not easy. The tension created a constant knot in her neck and shoulders.

Then there was the greater spiritual tension. God nudged at her conscience.

Did Nash have a right to know about his son? Would he want to know? And the worst question of all, was she holding back the information out of anger and bitterness? She couldn't deny its existence. Nash had hurt them badly, broken their hearts and their bank account all at once.

And he'd never even apologized.

If not for Poppy's insistence that she say nothing about the lost money, she'd ask Nash outright. Why had he let this happen to them? Didn't he feel even a smidgeon of remorse? Was money such a casual thing for him that he gave no thought to losing huge amounts?

Harlow dropped her head back and rolled her shoulders, the unanswered heartache and too much responsibility intruding on her thoughts of peace.

The problem of Nash. Poppy and Monroe incapacitated.

Another mortgage payment due in three days.

She blew out a long, fretting breath.

And now, whatever was wrong with the water system required attention sooner rather than later.

She had little choice but to sell something.

Once or twice, she considered asking Nash for a loan, but quickly dismissed the thought. Poppy would die of humiliation.

Raising her face to the sky, she prayed, "Lord, do you see me down here? Even with all the mistakes I've made, the Bible says You're an ever-present help in times of trouble."

She took up the rake and began to rake loose hay into a pile.

Something in her peripheral vision drew her attention.

Even as she sighed, her traitorous heart leaped.

The biggest problem of all headed in her direction.

Chapter Nine

If ever a man epitomized athletic grace, it was Nash Corbin. Every muscle in his body rippled with fluid ease as he jogged toward her. He didn't look as if he'd ever been sick a day in his life.

But he had been. The way he'd ignored the needs of his own body to help Poppy touched a tender place inside her.

As much as she chastised herself for staring, Harlow watched in admiration as Nash's long, strong legs smoothly ate up the space between them. He was reputed to be one of the fastest men in the NFL. Today he only jogged, but his long stride covered the ground quickly.

Her stomach tightened, and if those were butterflies dancing around in there, she'd kill them with an overdose of Pepto Bismol.

She did not want to find Nash attractive.

But she did. Oh, she did. More than ever.

Blast his eyes and his bad shoulder and all his other overly good-looking parts.

He still had a powerful effect on her, not just because he was dynamically fit and handsome, but because of the memories between them. She couldn't forget the wonderful man he'd been, the man she'd loved.

So much about him was the same. And yet, there was the long silence, the devastating investment scheme that had nearly ruined her and her family.

And still not a hint of remorse from him.

She dug the rake into the ground with a little more force than necessary.

Why did he insist on jogging in the direction of her house? Why couldn't he run on his own property? Or, if he was so desperate to maintain his privacy, why not stay in his house and jog in place? The weather was cold and wet, for crying out loud! Only a short time ago, he'd been sick enough to pass out.

He raised a hand in greeting. Harlow hunkered down inside her jacket and kept raking without returning the wave.

They were no longer close friends. He was not her best buddy anymore. At least, that's the lie she told herself. But after the days spent caring for him, visiting, talking and joking, it felt like it.

The little voice inside her head grew louder. He

was the father of her son. Their son. Nash was far more than a good friend, even if he didn't know it.

The inner pressure to tell him reared its head. She fought the urge. Wouldn't everyone be better off to leave well enough alone?

Clearly, his career was the most important thing in his world. All Nash talked about was getting well and getting back to work. He was doing everything in his power to make that happen.

Yesterday, she'd spotted him from the truck when she'd counted cows near his ranch. He'd been running then, too, only he'd set up some kind of obstacle course to maneuver. Old tires to run through. Saw horses to jump over.

Nash had never been lazy. He'd be fit again in no time, heading back to Florida, back to his beloved career, his fancy life and his big money, and his wildly enthusiastic fans.

He'd forget all about the Mathesons. Again.

Wouldn't it be a terrible thing to give Davis a father only to have him go away?

Though every cell in her foolish body yearned toward the athlete, she would not allow him to hurt her or her family, especially her baby boy.

"Morning." Nash's grin and sparkly brown eyes caused a tickle in her chest.

Harlow paused, rake in hand. "You're obviously feeling good."

He was barely winded from the run.

Nash opened the gate and entered the lot, letting the silver barrier clang shut behind him. "How's Gus?"

"He says he feels like the frazzled end of a misspent life."

Nash laughed, white teeth flashing against his warmly tanned skin. He hadn't shaved this morning and the dark, scruffy beard was wildly attractive. "He's better."

Moving to the horses still ripping at the compressed hay, he ran a hand over Drifter's neck. "Thanks for looking after my boy."

Harlow flinched at his use of "my boy."

"No problem. He seems to remember me."

"Horses have long memories."

So did she. Nash, on the other hand, seemed to remember only what served him.

"Your saddle is in the tack room if you're up to riding him home."

"Later." He rubbed gloved hands together. "What are you doing? How can I help?"

"You didn't come over here to work."

"I'm pretty sure I did. Feeling good, could use the exercise."

"I don't need you."

"Ouch." He clutched a hand to his impressive, blue-hoodie-covered chest as if her words stung.

In spite of her conflicted emotions, Harlow grinned. "Poor baby. So needy. Wa-wa."

Nash's handsome face crinkled with humor. "There's the sassy Harlow I know. Now, put me to work. I told you'd I'd help out over here as soon as I could."

"You are rehabbing a surgical shoulder. I won't be responsible for interfering with the healing process of the NFL's most valuable player."

"You won't be. I will. Working out is good for me."

She leaned the rake against the fence and shoved both hands into her pockets. "Why don't you go back to Florida where you have team doctors and rehab equipment and whatever pros use to heal up fast."

"Trying to get rid of me?"

"Maybe."

He laughed as if she joked. She didn't.

"I'm serious, Nash. There's nothing for you here. Why come back home after all this time?" She shouldn't have said home. His home was Florida. This was the place he'd dumped as fast as his speedy legs could escape.

His handsome mouth tightened, and Harlow saw worry in those dark eyes. He fisted a hand on one hip and looked to the side, staring out across the brown grassy fields.

Had she hit a nerve?

She didn't want to care.

"Lots going on in my life right now, Harlow. I needed time to think, sort out some problems."

"Your shoulder will heal, Nash." Reassuring him seemed to ooze from her DNA. She simply couldn't help herself. "The team won't replace you. You're too valuable."

He shook his head. "It's not only that. It's more...personal stuff."

Oh. Personal. As in a woman. Or several women.

She was not about to ask for details.

Her chest pinched. She swallowed her disappointment.

Foolish, foolish woman. Would she never learn?

Taking up the rake again, she started clearing the area of horse manure. Animals made a habit of leaving gifts after she fed them.

A powerful hand reached out and took the implement away. "I got this. Go inside. Grab a coffee break and warm up."

"It's not that cold today."

He shook his head and kept raking, though he was, she noticed, careful to give most of the work to his uninjured side.

"Does it hurt?" There she went again. Caring too much. Fixer of problems, except for her own.

"Not too much anymore. Hurt like crazy when it first happened."

"How did you get injured? In a game, I'm guessing."

He shot her amused glance. "I'm crushed that you don't watch my games, but since you apparently don't, I took a blindside hit. Targeting foul."

Hackles rose on her back. "Someone hit your shoulder on purpose?"

She sounded every bit as incensed as she felt.

His bottom lip quirked. "I don't like to think so, but he's a guy known for playing dirty. He'll sit out a game for it."

"While you sit out for weeks or months." The incident made her furious. She wanted to chase the guy down and…do something drastic. "That's not fair at all!"

Nash leaned the rake against the fence. "You look fierce. The same way you did when Pamela Shaffer broke up with me in front of half the school and walked off with Brent Ramsey."

"The student council president. I remember that. I was so mad I wanted to snatch out every strand of her fake blond hair. She was mean."

"Good thing I found that out." He made a tsking sound. "But she sure looked pretty in her little cheerleader outfit."

Harlow whacked him on the arm. His good one. He rubbed it and groaned, pretending pain. "You hit pretty hard. For a girl."

His mouth curved upward when he said "for a girl."

She whacked him again—barely—and they both laughed.

Laughing with Nash felt good.

He tossed his arm around her shoulders the way he'd done many times when they were growing up. "Come on, Matheson. Let me buy you a cup of coffee. Then, I'll help you finish the chores."

Harlow stiffened and slid from beneath his warm, too-comfortable, too-familiar arm. Getting cozy with Nash was a fool's game.

"I told you. I don't need your help. Just go."

She grabbed the rake and held it between them like a shield.

Nash's good humor faltered. He raised both hands in surrender. "Guess I'll go inside and say hello to Gus then. Does he still like to play checkers?"

He loved to. "I'm not sure he's up to it."

That was only partially true. Poppy was bored from inactivity. He would love company. And he loved playing checkers. He'd been the one to teach her and Nash the rudiments of the game. He and a neighbor played either chess or checkers about once a week, except Gene wasn't available at present. He was visiting his new grandson in Idaho.

Eyes narrowed as if he could see inside her brain, Nash gave her a long, searching look before saying, "Won't hurt to ask."

He turned toward the house.

"Nash." Her brain was a jumbled mess. She wanted him to go away. But his arm around her had felt wonderful. She liked him. She despised him.

Oh, Lord, why have You sent this trouble my

way? Are You trying to teach me something? If so, can we just get it over with and move on?

She could practically hear Poppy's voice reminding her that holding a grudge was wrong. Turn the other cheek. Show kindness.

Was that God's answer, too?

Poppy had loved Nash like a son, and he needed the company.

Playing checkers with Davis wasn't much competition, especially since Poppy let him win at least half the games. Losing a few, though, was good for the boy. Taught him that life doesn't give you everything you want.

Man, was that true.

She loved her family, enjoyed the animals and ranching. Had plenty of friends though she had little time for them lately. She enjoyed her church, loved God and was trying to learn and grow in her knowledge of Him.

But something was definitely missing.

She knew what it was, even if she had given up hope of ever being loved by a good man. Since Davis's birth, she'd had exactly three dates. One a year for every year of her son's life. Dates that had absolutely no spark.

The only spark she'd ever experienced stood in her barn lot as unattainable now as he'd been four years ago. Still sparking.

Oh heart. Why do you betray me?

She looked from the handsome athlete to the

back door, uncertain. Why was she worried? Nash had met Davis. He'd accepted her explanation about Davis's father.

Could the worry be for herself, for the sparks and butterflies and rapid pulse she couldn't seem to control?

Both hands inside his hoodie pouch, Nash quietly waited for her to speak her mind, his warm, dark eyes questioning.

She fought an inward battle, realizing she could not explain her rude behavior.

Finally, she said, "Be prepared to lose."

A quick grin flashed and he headed inside.

Heart thundering like an Oklahoma storm, Harlow returned to her chores and hoped that she could, somehow, survive until he went back to Florida.

Nash studied the checkerboard, contemplating his next move, an untouched cup of coffee to his right. Gus insisted on the providing the beverage, but Nash's stomach wasn't quite there yet.

The older man sat up straight in his recliner, the checkers table pushed close enough to reach.

Gus's color was better, and he was feisty today. Occasionally, he rubbed his hands together in glee. Right before he jumped one of Nash's checkers.

Nash pinched his upper lip between finger and thumb, concentrating.

"Might as well give up, my man," Gus said, with a hint of delight. "You're toast."

"Not so fast." He jumped one of Gus's checkers. "Crown me."

"I was hoping you wouldn't see that."

Nash jacked an eyebrow. "Trying to psych me out?"

"Name of the game. Distract the opponent and he'll falter." Gus took two more of Nash's checkers. "Like that."

"Hey!"

The older man chortled. Nash shook his head, smiling, refreshed by the simple game of checkers with a friend. After the strange conversation with Harlow, he needed to clear his mind.

She blew hot and cold, as if she hated him one minute and was his friend the next. Except Harlow was no longer the old pal he remembered. She was…more. Maybe she'd always been more and he'd been too football-focused to recognize the signs.

Given the mess he was in, falling for his neighbor was not a good plan.

Refocusing his thoughts on the checkers game, he pretended to sip his unwanted coffee and studied the board. Gus was right. He was toast. Nothing he could do to win this game. Unlike football when wild changes could occur in the final two minutes, the writing was on the wall.

He moved his remaining king into the fray,

knowing he was giving up, which wasn't like him at all.

Harlow's little boy sprawled on the living room floor, the collie close by, rolling Hot Wheels back and forth on the carpet. He made motor sounds and occasionally, with much gusto, crashed two cars together in a resounding explosion. Each time, the dog raised her head to be sure the child was okay. Nash and Gus exchanged glances and chuckled, and the boy glanced up and grinned. Such a cute kid. Sweet dog too.

Monroe hobbled through the living room a couple of times and flicked a look their way, a scowl on her face. At least the portion of her face that he could see behind the long fall of thick hair. She was still pretty, though clearly self-conscious about the facial scars. Twice, she tried to lure Davis upstairs to play Legos, but he wanted to stay with the "manses."

The game ended and Gus rested back against his chair. "Nap time. Tuckered out by a little game of checkers. Aggravating."

"I hear you."

Gus sniffed. "I guess you do. You're looking pert now, though."

"Almost back to myself."

"How long you reckon you'll be around, Nash? Getting healed up, I mean."

"Not sure. Got some thinking to do before I go back. And I'd like to help out around here a little.

Payback. But Harlow seems dead set against letting me do anything."

Something changed in Gus's expression, an odd look, a cautionary shift as if he wanted to say something and held back.

What was that about?

"Don't tell her I said this. She's mule-headed sometimes. So, I'd count it a favor if you'd just jump in and do what you can to help out. She'll fuss and spit a little but keep at it. She works too hard, takes on the whole load, though we haven't given her a lot of choice lately with the lot of us gimpy as a two-legged spider."

"You can't help it, Gus, any more than I could stop that alligator in my guts." He smiled a little. "I've noticed Harlow's long hours. Sometimes I see the truck lights in the field long after dark."

Another of the reasons he never wanted to ranch again. The work never ended. Cattle didn't take vacations. If they calved or got sick or hung up in barbed wire or out on the road, day or night, cold or hot, rain or scorcher, a rancher was on the job.

"Yep. Yep. Good girl, my Harlow." Gus rubbed a finger and thumb over his white mustache. "Carries the world on her shoulders, that one does. Thinks she has to take care of everyone and everything."

"I guess that comes from losing her parents so young."

"And coming to live with an old man who didn't know the first thing about three heartbroken little girls. Harlow was only twelve, but she mothered Monroe and Taylor, took responsibility for them. And for me. That girl taught herself to cook so's I wouldn't have to. She'd get up an hour early before school and make breakfast for her sisters and me. Did you know that?"

He didn't.

Nash rose from the ottoman he'd perched on. "She once told me she was afraid you'd get tired of them if they were too much trouble and send them away, so she tried to take care of the younger ones and make your life easier."

"I didn't know that. A right shame. Good she had you to talk to, I guess." Again, an odd expression passed over the old man. Eyes squinted, he stroked his long, white mustache a couple of times before speaking. "The two of you used to be thick as horse flies in June. For a time, I was hoping you and her…" Gus waved a bony hand. "She sure enough put a lot of stock in you back then."

Back then. But not now. Was that what Gus meant?

Nash's fault. Like every other idiotic thing he'd done in the past four years.

Uncomfortable with the shift in conversation, he said, "Grab that nap, Gus, but you owe me another checker game."

Gus chortled. "Didn't get enough whooping, huh?"

The little boy leaped to his feet. "I play. I play." Davis patted his chest with his small hands. "Can I play?"

Nash glanced from the child to Gus.

The old man nodded. "Play the boy, Nash. He knows how. Just needs direction here and there."

"Is that right?" To the bright, sweet face he said, "You want to play checkers?"

An eager nod was his answer.

Other than the children of friends and teammates, Nash had not spent extended time in the company of kids, but he visited lots of children's hospitals. This was Harlow's child, which made him extra special.

"Hop up here, Davis." Nash patted a chair seat. "I'm a little rusty with checkers. You promise not to beat me too badly like your Poppy did?"

The sweetest giggle pealed from Davis's throat. Light brownish-green eyes, so like Harlow's, sparkled with fun and just the right amount of boyish orneriness. A dimple flashed on his left cheekbone, directly below the eye.

Nash stilled, frowned. The dimple looked familiar.

Real familiar.

He brushed away the thought.

A cheekbone dimple in that exact spot was unusual, but not rare, was it? Just because Nash's own mother sported one in the same place didn't mean the two of them were related.

Why couldn't he get that idea out of his head? Harlow had already explained about Davis's parentage.

Yet, it haunted him.

Gus popped the handle on his recliner and tilted back, his eyes closed, a soft smile visible beneath his mustache.

Davis started to chatter about red being his favorite color. Except for blue. And purple.

Glad for the distraction, Nash pushed the red checkers in his direction.

Handsome kid. Friendly. Smart.

Davis glanced at Gus and put a tiny finger to his lips. "I has to be quiet. Poppy's hurt. I prayed for him."

Nash nodded, his chest pinched at the thoughtful gesture.

Whoever fathered Davis was a foolish man for letting go of Harlow and the boy.

Nash hoped it wasn't him.

Chapter Ten

Harlow shucked her boots and coat at the back door and then stopped at the kitchen sink to wash her hands. The faucets gurgled and coughed before spitting out a limited amount of water. The situation grew worse by the minute.

From the nearby laundry room, the smell of laundry detergent wafted in. She heard the *whump-whump* of spinning washer and dryer.

Harlow dropped her head back and groaned.

Monroe was determined to be useful, and Harlow had forgotten to ask her not to do laundry today. Even though her sister couldn't carry a clothes basket, she'd worked out a system of tossing dirty clothes over the stair railing. Then she and Davis scooted them into the laundry space on the other side of the kitchen.

Later, Harlow would carry the folded laundry upstairs and put it away. Their system wasn't perfect, but it worked until Monroe's leg healed and Poppy was back on his feet.

However, laundry could wait until the water issue was resolved, something that couldn't be put off much longer.

She'd have to schedule the well service call today.

Repairmen expected to be paid.

Still listening to the telltale gurgle from the washing machine, Harlow squeezed her eyes shut and prayed.

"Help me do what I have to do."

The choice would not be easy, but few things were. A woman, a mother, did what she had to do to care for her family.

As Harlow dried her hands and considered a drive to nearby Centerville, she heard Nash's deep, manly voice. Davis's small, childish one followed. Her precious baby boy.

Taking the towel, she moved to the opening between living room and kitchen and leaned against the door frame to peek inside. The scene filled her chest with the strangest sense of rightness.

Poppy was kicked back in his recliner asleep.

Nash and Davis hovered over the coffee table, playing checkers. The big athlete and the small boy. Father and son.

Her heart ached a little.

"I think you've got me," Nash said. "I see a couple of empty red squares. Do you?"

His index finger hovered over the empty spaces, broadly hinting.

Davis, little face screwed up in concentration, studied the board. So did Harlow. Nash was patiently teaching her son—their son—showing him how to find the moves himself. The child was too little to see them on his own. Too little to even play checkers except Gus had perched him on his lap to watch since Davis was big enough to sit up.

"Here?" Davis pointed to the board, his eyes on Nash.

"Good job."

Davis's eyes lit up. Tongue between his teeth, he made the two jumps.

Nash groaned and made a good show of loser's despair. "Ah, man. You beat me!"

Grinning, Davis asked, "Can we play again?"

Harlow stepped into the room. "Not now, Davis."

Nash's head whipped around. "Hey. I didn't hear you come in."

"Nap time for Davis. Poppy tends to forget on purpose and then this little cowpoke is cranky as a bear by bedtime."

Davis's formerly happy countenance turned sour. He stuck out his bottom lip. "I don't want a nap."

"I do, I do." Nash waved his hand like a kid in school, making both Harlow and Davis chuckle.

"Listen, buddy, naps are awesome. They make you grow."

Davis's eyes widened. "Big like you?"

Harlow's heart bumped. Quickly, she said, "As big as God wants you to be."

Holding out a hand, she led him to the staircase. "Up you go. Auntie's working at her desk, but she'll put on your music for you."

She hugged and kissed her son and watched him plod up the steps, his legs showing no indication of ever being as long as his father's. Yet.

But they probably would be.

Nash hadn't hit his growth spurt until late middle school. Then, practically overnight, he'd become the tallest boy in school.

Seeing her son interact with his birth father opened up a can of worms she'd ignored until now.

Someday Davis would be old enough to ask questions.

Then what?

What would she tell him about his father?

Nash observed the expression on Harlow's face as she watched her son trudge up the stairs. He knew that look. The corner of her bottom lip caught between her teeth. A slight pull between her eyes.

Something worried her. Something about the little boy.

Which brought him right back to the niggling at the base of his brain. Who was Davis's father? The boy was somewhere past three years old. Nash had been away four. The timing was right. Davis's left cheekbone bore the mark of an unusual dimple, exactly like the one on Nash's mother's face. The boy had a cowlick in the same spot Nash had battled all his life, which was one of the reasons he kept his hair short.

Nash swallowed hard. If he was Davis's father, he wanted to know.

Harlow claimed he wasn't.

Or had she?

Slowly, while mulling, he replaced the checkers in their case.

He tried to recall Harlow's exact words. Something about her and the guy being together only a short time before he left.

With a start, he realized that nothing in her statement ruled out Nash as the boy's dad.

He cleared his throat. "Harlow."

She whipped around, startled. "I forgot you were here."

One side of his mouth lifted. "No, you didn't."

Her eyes narrowed. She tilted her head to one side. "Oh, that's right. You're unforgettable."

Snarky again. Defensive. Not joking the way she used to. He was beginning to think her bad attitude was about more than his four-year silence.

"I want to ask you something."

Caution leaped into her eyes. She reached for the checkers box on the table. The pieces inside rattled. “I need to put this away.”

He put his hand over hers, stopping her jittery movements. “Harlow.”

She lifted hazel eyes to his. Her throat flexed. “What?”

Gus shifted in the recliner, mumbled in his sleep.

The older man was in the room. The timing was wrong. Nash wanted to ask her, but not here, not now, not without thinking things through.

If she said, yes, what would he do or say?

Knee-jerk reactions were seldom good. He’d sure learned that the hard way of late.

He shook his head and tamped back the question pressing to be released.

Clearing his throat again, he asked the next thing that came into his head. “Mind if I use your computer?”

His finances were never far from his thoughts. Some part of him kept hoping he’d been wrong, that his accounts remained intact. He needed to take a look.

As if she’d expected some other topic of conversation, Harlow blinked a couple of times before saying, “Regretting the cell phone you didn’t bring?”

Nash shrugged an eyebrow. “Not that much.”

The ranch computer was an older workhorse

desktop that sat on a small table at the end of the living room next to a two-drawer file cabinet, the Matheson version of a home office.

"Admit it. You're missing all your social media fans." This time her sarcasm was tempered with amusement.

"Desperately. They complete me." He intentionally joked, not wanting the cold-eyed Harlow to resurface.

His attempt at humor worked. She snickered and booted up the machine.

Nash liked that she saw him as an ordinary guy, not a superstar to fawn over. The attention of strangers had been fun at first. These days, it made him uncomfortable, especially now that he knew what his fans didn't.

The familiar Windows screen popped opened.

Leaning over his shoulder, Harlow motioned to the computer. "Internet is slow out here."

"I remember."

Nash logged into his web-based email, which immediately populated dozens of messages from his agent, his close friends, his coaches. Messages he didn't want anyone else to see, especially the ones from his agent.

He minimized the screen and turned toward Harlow.

Her face, friendly a moment ago, closed up. She backed away. "Sorry. Didn't intend to pry."

"No. It's not that." It *was* that. He needed to

read the emails, check his bank statement, his investments. All things that could reveal his desperate situation. "I, uh, well, finances, passwords. You know."

Her expression turned as cold as a January ball game in Green Bay. "Of course. Don't let me bother you. I have more important things to do anyway."

Harlow spun on her boot heel and trotted up the stairs. Five minutes later, she came back down, a small purse over one shoulder. Before Nash could say anything, she hurried out the front door without so much as a glance in his direction.

He'd offended her. And he couldn't explain.

Harlow drove into nearby Centerville, a larger town than Sundown Valley where no one would question what she was about to do. What she had to do.

She still fumed from the encounter with Nash. His comment about finances had shot through her like a poison arrow. He was still rich. The Mathesons were poorer than ever. Because of him.

This trip to Centerville proved that.

How could he seem so much like the man she'd always loved and still ignore the elephant looming between them?

"Lord," she prayed, as the car wound around the curves and over the high hills of the Kiamichi,

"I don't want to be angry. I want the easy friendship Nash and I used to have."

She paused, let her shoulders slump. "That's not true, and You already know it. I want more, and I'm afraid to let it happen. I'm afraid to tell him about Davis. I'm afraid of letting him break my heart again. Afraid of releasing this pent-up resentment over investing so much money in a deal Nash recommended. Afraid of losing even more than we already have."

So many fears. Sometimes she thought she'd been afraid her whole life.

She was afraid of losing the ranch, afraid of not being able to pay the mortgage. She was afraid of so much. And now this.

A verse she'd memorized to combat the constant, nagging anxiety came to her, loud and clear.

For God hath not given us the spirit of fear; but of power, and of love, and of a sound mind.

"I know, Jesus, but how do I get there from here?"

When no answer came, she pulled the Jeep into the parking lot of a Centerville strip mall and killed the engine.

Did she really want to do this?

Could she do this?

Taking the ring box from inside her handbag, she flipped the lid. Tears gathered behind her eyes, burned her nose.

"Mama," she whispered, rubbing her fingers across the beautiful wedding rings.

She'd had two choices. In the end, she'd chosen to give up the rings. Burr had been her other option, but she used him on the ranch every day. She needed him. The rings sat in a drawer, useless, benefiting no one.

Though she'd once dreamed of wearing them as a bride, that dream had long since died.

Practicality won over sentimentality.

"I'm sorry, Mama," she said.

Then, with shoulders set in determination, she exited the Jeep and went inside the jewelry shop.

Nash stared at the computer screen, his worst fears confirmed. He was more than broke. He was wiped out.

Fighting a groan, lest he awaken Gus, he contemplated his next move. He absolutely had to speak to Harlow about Davis and the possibility that he was the boy's father. He was here and that was numero uno. Yet, his financial situation desperately required his attention and the only way to resolve that issue was to head back to Florida ASAP.

He'd come home to the ranch like a runaway child to lick his wounds. Once here, he'd discovered he had more problems than he'd imagined.

Harlow was mad at him. Again. Talking to her about Davis wouldn't be easy with her defenses on high alert.

A car engine rumbled outside. The Jeep, he thought. Harlow was back from wherever she'd stormed off to.

Was she still angry?

Turning back to the computer, he logged out and wiped his history. Not that he expected Harlow to pry, but he was taking no chances. He was already humiliated enough. A man had his pride.

He waited, having heard the car door slam a couple minutes ago, but Harlow hadn't come inside the house.

Curious, he stepped outside to see if she needed help carrying groceries or whatever.

He spotted her, halfway to the barn, head down, shoulders slumped.

Was something wrong?

With a frown of concern and figuring the barn was the most private place on the ranch to talk, Nash headed in that direction.

His feet squished as he crossed the soggy grass.

Entering the barn, he paused, blinking in the dim light to search for her. She was nowhere in sight.

Then, from somewhere deep in the large barn, he heard a noise, a sound that gripped his heart.

Harlow, the strong, tough cowgirl, was crying.

Chapter Eleven

"Harlow? Where are you? Are you okay?"

At the sound of Nash's worried voice, Harlow spun her back to the stall door and clapped a hand over her mouth. Tears flowed over her fingers, but try as she might, she couldn't stop them. She didn't want anyone to see her like this, especially Nash.

Hiccupping, gulping, she attempted to squelch the sobs.

Suddenly, a pair of strong hands gripped her shoulders and turned her around. Slowly, gently, Nash drew her against his chest.

Maybe she should have resisted, but she couldn't. Didn't want to. Nash Corbin had been her shoulder to cry on for most of her life, and she'd been his. With that much history between them, turning to him now was only natural.

With a shuddering sob, Harlow buried her face into his fleece hoodie. He smelled of fresh air and Gus's coffee, his strong arms an anchor in her personal storm.

She shouldn't trust him at all, but in this moment, she did.

Tears, those stubborn beasts, kept coming.

"Go head and cry if it helps," he murmured. "It's just me."

Just Nash. Just the man she loved. She'd needed him and, this time, he was here. He hadn't been before, but today he was and she was grateful.

With a deep sigh as if he, too, needed the comfort, Nash rocked her back and forth in his arms. She curled her fingers in the neck of his hoodie, felt his keloid scar brush her skin and cried all the harder. She cried for the sold rings, for lost dreams, for the secret she'd kept locked inside for four years, and finally for the empty place Nash had left in her life.

For a while, his large hands rubbed soothing circles on her back. Then, he moved to her hair, smoothing the long strands over and over again as he murmured soft, incomprehensible assurances.

Harlow let herself rest in the sound of his voice, the safety of his strength.

Time and space seemed narrowed to this moment. She never wanted to leave the comfort of his embrace.

But duty and common sense pulled at her. She had responsibilities inside the house. The family must have heard her drive in. They'd be wondering about her by now.

It would not do for someone to come looking for her and find her crying in Nash Corbin's arms.

Emptied of tears, shaky and weak, Harlow eased away from him. Eyes burning, cheeks hot, she raked her sleeve across her face. She must look a fright. "Sorry. I didn't mean—"

"No." Nash stopped her with a gruff word. "Don't do that. Don't apologize. What's happened? Who hurt you? I'll tear their heads off."

His fierce assertion brought a tremulous smile, her heart soft as velvet because of his kindness. "I did it to myself."

Which wasn't exactly true but close enough.

He turned her hands up, scanned them and then looked her over. Concern creased his forehead, soothing a bruised place on her soul. "Are you injured?"

"Only my feelings." She slid her eyes away from his intense, probing gaze. If he looked close enough, he'd see too much.

In one corner of the stall, a moth dangled from a thin spiderweb. Harlow felt like the moth, her world precariously hanging by a thread.

"Tell me," Nash insisted, and tugged her close enough to place a hand on either side of her face and force her to look up.

Something sparked between them. An awareness, perhaps surprise, flashed across his face.

His lips parted.

He canted toward her and, for half a second,

Harlow thought he might kiss her. Which was madness on her part.

Instead, he used his thumbs to wipe away her tears while he studied her face. The earth seemed to shift beneath her.

Did he feel it? Or did his unexpected tenderness have her imagination running wild? She hadn't leaned on anyone in ages, and this was Nash in exactly the way she needed him.

Regardless of the grief he'd caused, Harlow remembered the good man he'd once been.

She sniffed, still teary and snuffling, but more composed.

"What's happened?" he asked again. "Tell me."

The story tumbled out. The money issues, the well service expense and the sold wedding rings. Later she'd question the decision to share her troubles, but at the moment, she needed a shoulder and his was wonderfully broad and strong.

Her emotions waffled all over the place. She was a mental disaster. Despising him, needing him.

She still loved this man. And he was here, tenderly inquiring, interested in her heartaches. Caring.

"Your mother's wedding rings?" He held each of her hands in his as they talked. "The antique ones? Is money that tight?"

She nodded.

"That stinks. I wish—" Nash made a frustrated sound and dragged her back into his arms.

She didn't resist, even as she wondered what his wishes might be.

He cupped her head in his hand and pressed her against him. She felt the brush of something on her hair. A kiss for comfort, perhaps? It was so like the Nash of old.

Being this close, the two of them alone, made her long for him all the more. He was the Nash she'd always loved, tender and compassionate.

Even the barn, her usual solace, the place she came to pray and cry, couldn't hide her from her feelings for Nash Corbin.

"Could I ask you something?" His voice rumbled in the quiet atmosphere.

Reluctant to leave his embrace but knowing it was the wise thing to do and aware of a certain tension springing up like weeds, Harlow moved slightly away. "What?"

"Since I arrived," he said, "as pathetic as I was and as kind as you've been, I've felt this push-pull attitude from you. One minute, you're my best friend and the next you look as if you could stab me through the chest with an ice pick."

The ramifications of the required explanation rolled around in her head. Davis. The investments. Eventually, she'd have to tell him about Davis. The investments were on him.

Opting for a vague, nonreply, she settled for, "Did you have an actual question?"

His mouth tilted. "Always sassy. Harlow, I've missed you."

He'd said that a few too many times to believe.

She snorted, jerked her gaze away before his charm made her say things she'd regret. "No, you haven't."

He reclaimed her upper arms, holding them lightly with his fingers. "I'm sorry I stayed away so long."

"Me, too." *I loved you, you big galoot. Why didn't you call? Why didn't you come back? Why couldn't you love me, too?*

In the small space, he shifted, his broad arm brushing hers. He rotated to face her again, forcing the issue of eye contact, wearing an expression she couldn't comprehend, yet that soft look in his eyes increased her pulse.

Foolish, foolish woman.

Nash swallowed, parted his lips to speak, but seemed to change his mind and took a step back instead.

"When do you ever take a break, Harlow? Do something fun?"

That strange light in his expression had been about having a good time?

"I have fun." Turning to the stall corner, Harlow freed the helpless moth. It fluttered to the window and landed there, exhausted from its struggle. She understood its exhaustion. Would blurting everything free her in the same way?

"When?"

The question stumped her. The last time she'd had any real enjoyment was at Christmas watching Davis tear into his gifts.

"In case you haven't noticed, I run a ranch, care for my child, and two members of my household are hobbled. I'm busy."

"You are. So, let me fix dinner for you at my place tonight."

"What?"

"You heard me. You, me, a couple of grilled steaks. Kick back and relax."

"You don't have any steaks."

"I will have if you'll go into town and get them for me." He grinned the grin that always made her smile in return. Boyish, charming, persuasive. "And one of those packaged salads and some dinner rolls?"

Harlow's short laugh burst forth, half-disbelief, half-amusement. A few minutes ago, she'd been crying her eyes out, and now she was laughing.

Nash possessed the strangest power to make her feel both passionate anger and exuberant delight. "In other words, you want me to bring dinner to your house."

"I'll cook. And pay. You relax." He stopped, frowned, held up one finger. "I think I still have enough money to pay."

He said the words as if he actually doubted his ability to pay.

"You mean cash money?"

"Right. Cash. I don't carry much cash."

Most people didn't these days, and he certainly didn't want her using his credit or debit card. The whole town would know in minutes that Nash Corbin was back.

She tapped his impressive chest with her index finger. "Then, you'd better dig under the couch cushions like we did as kids because I'm coming over for steak dinner and you're paying, mister."

Surrounded by dark, scruffy whiskers, Nash's smile flashed. He pulled her into another of his easy hugs. Gentle, friendly, warm. Really warm.

Harlow drew in a long, relaxed sigh, and hugged him back.

Her neighbor felt wonderfully familiar. Like memories and good times and a friend to lean on.

As she stood in the smelly, cold barn gently enveloped in his powerful arms listening to the thud of his giant heart, Harlow knew—oh, yes, she knew—it was too late to keep her own heart safe from Nash Corbin.

That afternoon, Harlow once again drove Monroe's Jeep, this time to the grocery store in Sundown Valley. Davis came along for the ride and the hope of scoring a pack of gummy bears.

She still ached from the decision to sell Mama's jewelry and the trip provided a much-needed distraction.

Nestled deep in the Kiamichi Mountains, Sundown Valley was a typical, friendly small town where everyone knew everyone, at least by name. Surrounded by wilderness, lakes, forests and low, rolling mountains, the town was remote but thriving, due to a determined population. Even though they lived on the outskirts, Harlow's family was involved in local events, church and Friday night football games such as those Nash had starred in.

Driving down Main Street, she approached the Bea Sweet Bakery, a favorite hangout when she was a teenager. Today, the business produced light meals and delectable sweets. Cakes, cupcakes, sweet rolls. Pie. Nash loved pie.

When the thought struck, she pulled against the curb and took Davis inside to buy dessert for tonight's dinner, a rare treat, but Nash could afford it. She added a cinnamon roll for Poppy, a bear claw for Monroe and a blue frosted cupcake for Davis.

Ms. Bea, the bakery owner, asked about Monroe's leg and Poppy's injuries as she settled up the bill. The woman had her finger on the pulse of the entire county.

Winking, the baker tucked an extra cinnamon roll in the bag. "Tell Gus that one's payback."

Harlow tilted her head. "For?"

Bea laughed. "He'll know. Tell him I'll drive out Sunday after church if he's up for a visit."

Did Poppy have an admirer? She liked to think so, especially if the admirer was a nice, Christian lady like Bea Cunningham. As part of the same Bible study group, the pair saw each other every week.

Harlow left the bakery, stopped at the newspaper office to buy Poppy a paper and then headed to the grocery store.

Nash, whether by accident or design, had given her something besides her own trouble to think about. His invitation and request that she shop for steaks kept her too busy to dwell on the sold rings. It was done. Time to stiffen the spine and move on.

Change the things you can. Accept the things you couldn't. Good advice, she thought.

The key was to know the difference between the two.

Which was where she waffled. The issue of Davis and Nash was never far from her thoughts.

As she pushed Davis around the IGA in the grocery cart, filling it with Nash's order and a few items of her own, she ran into numerous people she knew. That was one of the pleasures of small towns.

Nash was fortunate no one had discovered his presence.

When a lanky cowboy rounded the end of an aisle and almost wiped her out, they both laughed. He touched the brim of his hat.

Wade Trudeau, owner of the area's largest ranch, pushed a basket brimming with groceries.

"How you doing, Harlow? I see you're traveling in fine company today." He tapped the top of Davis's hand. "Hi, Davis."

"And you're out and about all alone." A long-time single dad of triplets, Wade had recently married a sweet teacher from Tulsa.

"The perks of a great wife and a big family." He held up a list written in a feminine hand. "I volunteered for grocery duty. I had to come to the farm store anyway so why make two trips? Monroe still laid up?"

"Hobbling around. Poppy joined her."

Concern drew his eyebrows together. "What happened?"

She told him. "The tractor's still on its side in the pasture."

"Bowie and I can take care of that for you."

"I hate to ask."

He waved off her feeble protest. "You didn't. Consider it done."

Another benefit of small town living.

They parted ways, Harlow's spirits lifted by Wade's simple kindness. One less thing on her worry list.

A short time later, she drove up the still muddy driveway to her home, splattering mud, and parked the Jeep. After unbuckling Davis from his car seat, she handed him the smaller bakery sack and began unloading the groceries.

"Good timing." Nash crowded his big, attractive body next to hers and reached for the bags.

She hadn't seen him coming. Why was he even still here?

"Good timing for what? It's not dinnertime."

He pumped his eyebrows. "Come on. I'll show you."

Curious now, she grabbed the bag of potatoes and the bottle of laundry detergent and followed him into the house. After he'd deposited the groceries, he exchanged conspiratorial glances with Gus, and guided her back outside.

"What is going on?" she asked, chuckling at his secretive behavior.

"Gus said I could."

Harlow snorted. "You sound like an eleven-year-old."

"Remember the fun we used to have on that tire swing Dad built in my yard?"

"You'd spin me until I cried uncle."

"Oh, no, lady, that was you, spinning poor little gullible me until I nearly threw up. You wouldn't let me off."

"True. You were so wimpy." She widened her eyes, teasing. Nash was anything but wimpy.

"Close your eyes." He took her hand. "Go on, close them. It's not a trick. Trust me. I won't steer you wrong."

At that completely untrue statement, Harlow almost backed out. But Nash exuded charm, and he was obviously excited about something fun, so Harlow closed her eyes, covering them with one hand.

He slipped a muscled, rock-hard arm around her waist. She couldn't stumble if she wanted to. He was that solid, that strong.

The barn episode flashed in her mind. Nash, comforting her.

She'd once trusted him with her whole world.

"Making a turn to the right," he said. "Stop here for the big reveal."

"Am I on HGTV?"

He laughed. How she loved his rich, throaty, masculine laugh. The sound rumbled from deep in his chest.

"Open your eyes."

She did. Her heart *kerplunked.* Her eyes misted.

From the massive sycamore tree on the south side of the house hung an old-fashioned tire swing. Exactly like the one they'd played on as kids.

Why had he done that? Out of kindness? Nostalgia? Boredom? Was he trying to make up for past mistakes in some small way?

Or was this like the dinner invitation, a sympathetic gesture to ease her grief over the sold rings?

How did she stop caring too deeply for a man like that?

Davis would love the swing. *She* loved it and the sentiment it represented.

Oh, Nash. You're breaking my heart all over again.

"What do you think? Do you like it? Do you think Davis will like it?"

He sounded like an eager boy.

"It's perfect. I've wanted to get him a swing set, but—" She let the truth slide away. She had no money for large yard toys.

Spontaneously, Harlow circled his waist with her arms and hugged him. "Thank you."

His powerful arms embraced her in return, and she rested her ear against the logo on his hoodie.

Twice in one day. Or was it three times? Being this close to Nash was getting to be a habit she liked too much.

Nash holding her. Doing something nice for her and her son. His son.

He'd built a toy for his son, and he didn't even know it.

Oh, the irony.

Tears gathered in her eyes. The need to tell him about Davis pushed in.

Fear and worry and what-ifs followed.

He shifted slightly but didn't move away. If anything, his embrace shifted too, changed, gentled, moved slightly closer. He rested his chin on her hair.

"You like it," he whispered in a satisfied voice.

Why was he whispering? They were outside, no one around but the dog.

She nodded. "Love it. Love..." She'd almost said, *Love you too.*

"Good. I wanted to make you happy. To see

you smile again. You work and worry too much. I hate seeing you cry."

They remained in each other's embrace for longer than was probably prudent, but he made her feel the way she'd once felt with him. Safe, cared for, important.

Slowly, almost as if he was as reluctant to move as she, Nash eased back to look down at her. "Want to give it a whirl?"

"Will it hold me?"

"Guaranteed. Double ropes. You first, then we'll give Davis a ride."

"He'll be wildly excited."

So was she.

Nash held the swing steady while Harlow climbed inside the cold rubber ring. In seconds, his epic strength had her flying through the air, an adult pendulum on a worn-out truck tire. She laughed. Shouted. Enjoyed Nash's return laughter.

Then, with a glint in his eyes, he caught the double rope and rapidly wound the contraption tighter than a spring.

An anticipatory squeak escaped Harlow.

"Ready?" he asked.

She clutched the sides of the tire. "No."

With a wicked chuckle, Nash gave the swing a mighty heave.

For the first time in ages, Harlow wasn't worried. She wasn't scared. She was a carefree kid again, all because of Nash Corbin.

Chapter Twelve

Later, as Nash marinated the steaks and prepared to impress Harlow with his grill mastery, he relived the day, feeling accomplished. Time with Gus, the sweetness of Harlow's little boy over a board game, but most of all, the rope swing with Harlow, and later Davis, had given him the best day he'd had in a long time. Since the Super Bowl win. Since before he'd discovered the discrepancies in his financials.

Harlow's tears, though, had about wrecked him. She'd sold her mother's treasured wedding rings. If her tears had wrecked him, her sacrifice shamed him. Every cell in his body wanted to give her all the money she needed. Six months ago, he could have.

He couldn't give her money, but he could make her laugh. He could grill steaks and reminisce about their childhoods and build a tire swing for her son.

He couldn't remember when he'd had silly, freewheeling fun like the hour on the tire swing. Listening to Harlow's giggles and squeals thrilled him. Like old times. Good old times that he'd let slip from his memories during his climb toward the top of the sports world.

Eventually, Davis had wandered outside, fresh from his nap. The boy expressed even more delight in the new toy than his mother had.

Davis.

Some of Nash's joy seeped out like air from a leaky tire.

Tonight, he'd tackle the question that would either change his life or ruin a friendship with Harlow. Maybe both.

But he had to ask.

After seasoning the steaks with plenty of garlic, salt and pepper, he set them aside to finish marinating while he lit the grill and put the foil-wrapped potatoes on to bake.

The weather was cool, but not frigid. Spring was sneaking up on them, slowly but surely. The weather was perfect for a cookout on the back porch. He wished he'd thought to have her buy s'mores ingredients. Harlow liked chocolate anything.

Nash never again wanted to see Harlow cry.

Feeling a combination of eagerness to see her and dread because of his multiple reasons for inviting her, Nash hit the shower, shaved, dabbed on a generous splash of cologne. Dressing in clean jeans and a black tee under a warm, maroon button-down, he checked out his image in the mirror.

"Not bad." He no longer looked as gray and lifeless as leftover gravy.

He gently rotated his shoulder. "Better there too."

Not healed but not as painfully useless as before.

As much as he dreaded it, he needed to get back to Florida with the trainers and nutritionists. More than that, he had to find an attorney he could trust. Sooner rather than later.

Unless he was Davis's father. Then everything changed.

A knock sounded at the door followed by the familiar, "Hey, it's me."

His pulse jumped. Harlow was here.

Nash hustled into the living room where Harlow wiped her feet on an old rug he'd placed beside the door. She'd spruced up a little too. Almost as if this was a date, which, in a way, he supposed it was.

Emotions buzzed around in his chest like honeybees.

A bright blue sweater, New York Giants' blue, set Harlow's gorgeous hair aflame and highlighted her peachy skin. He tried not to look her up and down, but his eyes wouldn't obey.

She'd always been cute. Maturity made her beautiful.

"I brought dessert." She lifted a white box. "Cherry pie from the bakery."

"Sweet. Literally." He made a face at his pathetic joke and confiscated the box. Had she remembered his love for pie? Or was the dessert a mere coincidence? He liked believing she'd remembered. "Come on in. Are you hungry? The steaks are ready to go on the grill."

"Whenever."

Harlow knew this house as well as her own and joined him in the kitchen. They worked side by side, intentionally bumping each other, teasing, complaining that the other took up too much room. In his case, that was true. Which meant he jokingly blamed her.

Harlow tossed the bagged salad into a bowl and added the packaged extras. He set two plates on the small, round table next to the window.

It was a good feeling. He and Harlow, together again. Tonight, she wasn't the prickly, unpredictable woman he'd dealt with during the weeks since he'd come home.

She was Harlow, his old pal. Except she was different, too, and he liked those differences.

Earlier in the barn, she'd needed his comfort and he'd felt ten feet tall to be able to give it. He'd been sorely tempted to kiss her. He'd settled for holding her, listening to her soft breathing, absorbing her tears and praying he could find a way to make her life better.

She'd responded sweetly, without the prickly attitude.

Apparently, he had broken through whatever wall she'd erected between them. He hoped things stayed that way.

Had she been guarded because of Davis? Was he the reason she'd run hot and cold whenever Nash came around? Was she afraid he would discover the truth and be angry that she hadn't told him?

He couldn't seem to get the boy off his mind and wouldn't until he'd asked.

But not yet. He wanted to enjoy Harlow's company again in case he ruined their friendship forever by prying into her private business.

But if it was *his* business too…

All this hashing and rehashing was making him a little crazy. He refocused on a search for paper napkins, which he didn't seem to have. No paper towels either.

"Wade Trudeau and his cousin, Bowie, are coming over tomorrow to move the tractor." Harlow pulled open a drawer and dug around until she found two steak knives.

He shot her a quick glance. "You didn't tell him about me—"

Holding the knives in one hand, she pointed them at him. "Don't worry. Your privacy has not been breached. You are safe from your hordes of adoring, ravaging fans."

The tension eased from him. He grinned, a little embarrassed that she thought that about him. "Sorry. My head is a weird place right now."

An expression he didn't understand crossed Harlow's face. She spun away, taking the knives to the table. "I know exactly what you mean."

She couldn't know what he meant. Which made him wander what she was thinking. Was it about Davis? His nerves jittered. And there he went again, fretting over the conversation ahead.

When the food was prepared, they sat at the small dining table next to a curtained window overlooking the yard.

"This looks great, Nash," she said. "Mind if I say grace?"

"Please. Go ahead."

He closed his eyes, silently praying for the evening ahead as she said a simple prayer of thanksgiving for the food.

"Amen," he said when she finished. "I've made a lot of mistakes recently and that's one of them."

She unfolded the tea towel he'd put out in place of the napkins he didn't have. "Letting your faith slide?"

"I found my old Bible in a box in the closet, been reading it."

"That's good, Nash. I'm glad. Having a relationship with Jesus has helped me a lot. I don't feel so alone anymore."

"Alone? You have a family under foot all the time." Her house filled with people was one of its draws when he was a boy. He'd loved the noise and movement and constant companionship with kids his age that was missing in his home. Being an only child stunk even if Mom and Dad claimed he was an answer to many heartfelt prayers.

He shook out his tea towel, identical to Harlow's, and placed it on his lap.

"It's not the same," Harlow responded. "You know how I am. I've always felt responsible for everything, as if I had to take care of the whole world."

"You were that way as a kid."

"Yes, I was. Still am to a certain extent, though I can't understand why. My sisters are grown. The ranch belongs to all of us, not just me, but it seems I'm the one to handle everything."

"You're in a tough spot right now. It'll get better when Monroe and Gus are back on their feet."

"I know. You're right. Poppy tells me to cast my cares on Jesus, like the Bible says, but I have a hard time doing that. I'm getting better though." She sliced into the juicy steak and he waited for her hum of approval. "It's a relief to know that Someone all-knowing and powerful is at my side to help out when I don't know what to do."

"It sure is." He filled his plate and offered her the salad. Times like this he needed God more than he'd ever imagined. With his life in such a mess, his head spun. Only God could see the big picture. He sure couldn't.

One thing for certain, he didn't want to mishandle tonight and ruin things forever between him and Harlow.

They ate in silence for a while except for occasional comments on the tender club steaks. She claimed they were delicious but not as tender as the Matheson grass-fed beef.

"Why aren't we eating your steaks, then?" How had he forgotten that most ranchers raised and processed their own meat? Had he become that much of a city boy in four years?

"Our freezer's nearly empty." She glanced up, eyebrows lifted in mischief. "And you were buying."

"Why's the freezer empty? Don't you usually keep a steer ready to go?"

She took a drink of water before replying, as if she needed to think before responding.

"We sold all our steers last fall."

The Matheson financial struggles must be bad, really bad. Worse even than he'd thought. Not that he was surprised. It was often a way of life for small-time ranchers. Except he didn't like thinking they might be in need and there was nothing he could do to help.

At least not at present.

He shoved in a bite of savory steak and let go of the topic. They had a more serious discussion ahead. No use stirring the waters over cattle prices.

As their hunger abated and the cherry pie was

served, Nash intentionally guided the conversation toward casual subjects.

He told her funny locker room stories and described his friends and teammates. She updated him on people they both knew. They talked about her baby sister, Taylor, now a young woman with an apparent lust for travel and adventure that kept Harlow on edge.

"You're a control freak." He aimed a forkful of cherry pie in her direction.

As long as he'd known Harlow, she'd needed to overprotect her sisters, her grandpa, her whole world. Sometimes even him. Because of her parents' deaths, which she hadn't been able to stop, perhaps she'd developed a need to keep everything and everyone around her safe and in order.

Her younger sister apparently had rebelled.

"I am not a control freak! Taylor's fragile. Flitting from one place to another with strangers is not safe."

"Strangers to you, Harlow, not to Taylor. She's a grown woman."

She stabbed a bite of piecrust with particular viciousness. "You wouldn't understand."

"Guess not." He quickly dropped the touchy subject. The last thing he wanted to do tonight was to put Harlow on the defensive. Things threatened to get heated enough later when he asked about Davis.

As the conversation bounced from one thing

to another, she asked to see his Super Bowl ring. He retrieved it from the glove box of his car, still hidden in the detached garage.

As she admired the ridiculously bejeweled ring, Nash realized, as much as he disliked the idea of selling, like Harlow, his valuable ring was one more thing he could sell to generate cash. If he had to.

Please, God, help me resolve his mess I'm in. Finances. Injury. Harlow. Davis.

He could hardly think straight for the pile of worries that kept growing higher.

Harlow waved a hand in front of his face. "Hey there, mister, where did you go?"

"Nowhere, just…admiring your pretty hair."

She touched a hand to the long strand lying across one shoulder. "Thank you. Remember when you called me fire stick and said I looked like a lit match?"

He tilted his head back and grinned at the popcorn ceiling. "We were ten."

"Eleven. Your mom overheard and made you apologize."

"She didn't know you called me Godzilla first after I stepped on your foot."

Harlow giggled. "Nearly broke my toe."

They exchanged smiles and the moment held, time suspended as if four years hadn't passed, remembering while also enjoying the moment. Being with Harlow felt right, comfortable in a way no other woman ever had. With her, he was completely himself.

"I'm stuffed." She pushed the remaining bites of cherry pie his direction. "Want this?"

Another habit of times past. Petite Harlow fed her leftovers to him, an ever-hungry, fast-growing teenager.

Nash finished off both pieces of pie and sat back. "That was good."

"Thanks for inviting me. I was reluctant at first, but I'm glad I came."

"Why? I mean, why reluctant?"

She hopped up from the table and began clearing their few dishes. Grilling meant easy cleanup. Plates clattered as she placed them in the stainless-steel sink.

He followed, anxious to talk to her about Davis but dreading it too. When she began rinsing the plates, he reached over and turned off the faucet.

"Leave these. There's something I want to talk to you about."

He handed her a clean tea towel. She dried her hands and carefully draped it over the oven handle.

"What?"

He took her hand, warm from the water, and tugged. "Come on. Let's sit."

She pulled back, expression cautious. "This sounds serious."

He recaptured the hand, enveloping the small, soft fingers in his giant paw. "It is."

Her gaze widened. She looked to one side and then around the room as if in search of escape. "We've been having such a nice time. I don't want to be serious."

"Please." He kept his tone quiet and cajoling. "It's important."

With a sigh of surrender, she dipped her head and followed him into the living room.

Harlow's pulse jacked to Mach speed as Nash tugged her down beside him on the old brown couch and took both her hands in his.

He looked as serious as a cracked skull.

A lump, thick as an apple, tightened her throat. She swallowed against it.

Whatever this was about, she had a feeling she wouldn't like it.

It couldn't be about Davis, could it? There was no way Nash could have guessed. Was there?

"What is it, Nash? You're making me nervous."

He drew in a breath, blew it out. "I don't know how to say this."

Warning jitters danced up her back. "Just say it."

"I don't want to upset you, and if I'm off base, I apologize in advance, but before I left for the NFL, we, uh, made a big mistake. At the time you said there were no, uh, repercussions."

She tensed. Here it came, the thing she'd dreaded since he'd passed out in her pasture.

What if he was angry? What if he hated her? What if he wanted to take Davis away?

Her insides began to shake.

"That was four years ago, Nash. We've moved on."

"Have we?" He speared her with intense eyes. "I need you tell me directly to my face. Is Davis my son?"

There it was.

Heat rushed up her neck and over her face. Her heart pounded so hard she thought it might come out of her chest.

She should have told him days, weeks, months, maybe years ago. But she'd been angry and disappointed in him. For years, she'd thought he neither wanted nor deserved Davis.

She still thought that might be true.

But, her conscience said, she still should have told him.

He had a right to know.

With barely a whisper, her mouth dry as cotton, she braced for his fury. "Yes."

He tilted backward, groaned and then dropped his head into his hands. "I am sorry. So very sorry. This is my fault. I was such a reckless, insensitive fool. None of this should have ever happened."

Harlow stiffened. "I will never regret having Davis."

Nash lifted stricken eyes to her face. "No. No. Never. He's a great kid. But my careless behavior that night has cost you so much. I should have been here for you. I should have followed up. You went through this alone."

His reaction was not what she'd expected.

Nash was beside himself with regret. Blaming himself, instead of her? It didn't make sense.

She had the oddest feeling that she should console him. After all he'd done to hurt her, she still loved him that much. Still wished he had been there when Davis was born, that he had loved her and their son.

"Nash, it's done. Can't be undone."

He rose from the couch and paced to the end of the room and back again, stopping in front of her. She lifted her chin and looked at him.

"This is on me, Harlow. My mistake. My selfish actions. I've wronged you and that little boy immeasurably. I have to change that. Let me make amends. We'll get married."

She blinked. Blinked again. Her mouth fell open. Had he just said what she thought she'd heard?

"Married?"

"I care about you. Always have. I think you feel the same. Right?" His hopeful expression baffled her. What on earth did he have to be hopeful for other than assuaging a guilty conscience?

Since she was fifteen, she'd dreamed of Nash's marriage proposal and yet, he'd tossed the offer out like an afterthought. Which it was. A spur-of-the-moment, let-me-fix-this afterthought.

No romance, no declaration of love.

None of the things she'd dreamed of.

That's because Nash didn't love her, never had. Love had nothing to do with this conversation. Not one thing.

He no more wanted to marry her than he wanted to live on this ranch and raise cattle.

Stunned into humiliated silence, her brain tried to make sense of his reaction.

The man actually thought he was doing the right thing.

Cushions gave way as Nash sat down again and patted her limp, lifeless hands. She felt too empty and shaken to move away.

He was sorry. He'd made a mistake. He regretted the "wrong" he'd done.

"It's the best we can do for now." He plowed ahead as if she'd agreed to his outlandish proposal. "We'll get married right away. Before I head back to Florida to...deal with some problems there."

Problems in Florida.

Probably a woman who'd be as heartbroken as she was.

The admission yanked Harlow to attention.

Nash was about to leave again, but he wanted to clean up the mess he'd left behind the first time.

She didn't know whether to be insulted or furious.

So, she was both.

The inner shaking worked its way to the outside. Shock and numbness gave way to anger. Blood surged with a roar into her temples, pounding there like a war drum.

"No." The denial exploded from her, a volcanic eruption.

Nash's words played over and over in her head. *Mistake. Wrong. Regret.*

His apology stabbed her through the heart. She didn't want an apology.

She wanted Nash's love, not his remorse.

Davis was a gift, not a mistake to regret.

Nash could save his self-reproach for the fact that he'd ruined her family financially.

The urge to throw *that* in his face rose up like a stomach virus. She fought it down, silenced by her promise to Poppy.

"Why not?" Nash's eyebrows dipped, his expression bewildered. "Marriage is the best solution. We're both single. Davis needs a dad. He's my son."

He had no idea that every loveless, insulting word ripped her to shreds.

"He's *my* son," she said through gritted teeth. "We were doing fine until you came along, and we'll do fine after you leave. I will not marry you."

"I don't understand. You're not making sense."

She jerked her hands free and stood up, looming over him the way he'd unwittingly done to her. "Of course, you don't understand. Because you are so special and important, rich and famous, why would any woman refuse your offer of marriage?"

She was starting to get worked up. Really worked up. Anger was better than the sheer devastation tearing through her.

"He's my son, Harlow. I want to know him. I'm sorry for—" he waved one hand as if to erase what he saw as a problem "—everything."

His calm voice added fuel to her fury. "You've apologized enough. Stop it. Just stop it."

He held up both hands in surrender, placating now.

"Okay. Okay. Please. Let's both calm down and talk sensibly. I won't pretend to understand what's going on in that head of yours, but think about Davis. I'm not a terrible man, am I? A flawed one, I'll admit, but not terrible."

"No, of course not. I never said that." Maybe she'd thought it, though, after the investment debacle. But lately? No.

More's the pity. Falling in love with him all over again was about the most lamebrained thing she'd ever done.

"Don't you want him to know me? Shouldn't he have that? A day will come when he'll ask, you know. Won't he be angry that I wanted to be part of his life and you refused? That you kept him from me?"

Harlow twisted her hands together, trying to clear her thoughts. His proposal had blindsided her. Since his arrival, she'd planned to tell him about Davis. In her own way. At some point. Before he left again.

The trouble was, tonight she'd come over for a simple dinner between friends. He'd sprung this on her out of the blue.

Drawing in a cleansing breath, she nodded, forced her tight shoulders to relax. "You're right. However, do *not* mention marriage again. I won't keep you from Davis. In fact, I want you to be part of his life, but if I ever marry, it will be for love, not obligation. *I* deserve that and so do you."

There she'd said it. She'd put love on the table, her nonnegotiable.

"All right. I understand. I think." He shook his head again, his expression sad. "I really am sorry, Harlow."

She stabbed a finger at the air. It trembled.

"Don't apologize again. Ever." She whipped around and fumbled for the doorknob. "Keep the rest of the pie. I'm going home now." She shot one final glance over her shoulder. "Thank you for the dinner."

He dipped his chin and started to say something, but she didn't wait around to hear.

Chapter Thirteen

Nash didn't sleep much that night.

Rising before dawn, he wandered around the house and then outside. A huge white moon cast shadows over the fields, and thousands of stars speckled the inky sky. He'd forgotten how vivid they were in the country.

He traced his finger along the Big Dipper and down the stars of Orion's Belt.

From the corner of his eye, he saw something move. Near the fence line, a lone coyote prowled the brown grassland.

Nash watched, ready to act if the predator approached Harlow's cows.

Slowly, going to a stealthy crouch, the coyote eased toward the dark shadows hovered together beneath a clutch of trees.

Coyotes were opportunists, a bane of farmers and ranchers. Another reason he never wanted to ranch or farm again, although, he had to admit, he enjoyed the tranquil privacy of his ranch. Another thing he'd let slip his mind.

When the coyote edged closer, Nash sprinted toward the cows. He waved his arms and shouted. "Hey. Get. Go!"

The coyote bolted, disappearing into the wooded area along the creek that ran behind his ranch as well as Matheson land. He and Harlow had spent many childhood hours playing in Lost Creek, escaping the summer heat, chasing tadpoles, fishing for perch.

Nash slowed his steps.

He should tell Harlow about the coyote. She'd need to keep an eye on the pregnant heifers and new calves. Older ones fended for themselves pretty well. Mamas in labor were particularly vulnerable.

Had Harlow been vulnerable without him nearby when Davis was born?

He had a son, and the knowledge settled over him in a good way. Maybe deep down he'd known the boy was his from the start.

Last night, he'd handled the conversation about Davis all wrong, but try as he might, he couldn't figure out what else he could have said.

He'd apologized and offered to marry her, to make Davis his legal son. Why had she gotten so angry about that?

She didn't know he was in financial trouble. So, his lack of money couldn't be the reason for her rejection. Harlow had never been the kind of girl who cared about a man's wallet.

He cared, though. He needed money if he was going to take care of them the way he should have always done.

Yesterday, she'd admitted to financial issues of her own. That she'd sold her mother's treasured rings bothered him a lot.

Somehow, he'd get his investments straightened out enough to support his son. He owed them that much. Fact was, he wanted to take care of them, shower them with everything they didn't have.

Harlow worked too hard. Half of the farm equipment was old and held together by baling wire.

Even if she wouldn't marry him, he'd find a way to make her life easier.

Nash rubbed a hand over his heart. Her rejection of marriage cut through him, hurting more than he'd thought possible.

She was Harlow. He cared about her. He wanted to make things right.

Why didn't she understand his good intentions?

Pausing by the gate between his property and hers, he leaned on the corner post to catch his breath, but mostly to think.

With the trouble in Florida and now this stunning news, he'd never been as rattled.

From here on this gentle rise in the Kiamichi

foothills, he could see the tall, outdoor security light in the Matheson yard. Every rancher had one to deter predators and illuminate late night trips to barns and sheds. He'd hauled and barn-stacked many bales of hay by security light. Night work proved cooler than scorching summer days.

Memories. He had plenty of them of this place, all tucked away and ignored in pursuit of a dream. Some not so good but plenty of good ones.

Lights came on in the Matheson house. Gus, probably. The older man had always been an early riser.

Had Harlow struggled with sleep last night the way he had?

He considered jogging across the field to have coffee with whoever was up this early, but thought better of it. Later, after they'd both had time to think things through, he'd ask Harlow again to marry him. It was the right thing to do. His daddy had taught him that a man took responsibility for his actions. He wanted to do that. If she'd let him.

He'd never given much thought to marriage until now. He'd been too busy, too focused on his career and making money. But the idea of marrying Harlow now didn't scare him. Being separated from her again, having her angry with him, knowing that he'd hurt her, those things shook him.

No matter what Harlow decided, Nash was determined to be a dad to his son. She wouldn't deny him that. She'd said so.

He trusted her word, though after she'd kept Davis a secret, he wasn't sure why.

Jogging back toward the house, he stopped at the barn and put out hay for his horse. Hay from Harlow's barn.

She'd always been a friend when he'd needed one.

And he'd failed her miserably.

He'd been outraged that some jerk had abandoned her and her baby, and all along, he'd been that guy.

Could she ever forgive him? Could he forgive himself?

He wished he had someone to talk to about his disaster of a life. Once upon a time, he'd have confided in her or his dad or even Gus.

In less than a month, his whole world had imploded.

With no phone, his teammate Zack wasn't even an option. Frankly, like the debacle with his agent and investments, the news about Davis was too personal to share even with a good friend like Zack. Someday, he would, but not until he and Harlow had come to terms.

As he left the barn lot, the first rays of morning sent a pink-gold glow across the horizon. In the distance, the ancient mountains drew his notice.

A Bible verse came to him. He couldn't quote

the exact phrasing, but he remembered the gist of it. A long time ago, after several financial setbacks, his mother had taped the verse to the kitchen cabinet as a reminder. She'd left the yellowing paper there for years, and he'd seen it every time he came in for a glass of water.

"Though the mountains shake and the hills tumble to the sea, God's love won't ever be shaken. Is that right, Lord?"

Maybe not, but the sentiment was correct. And the knowledge made him feel better. No matter how much he messed up or how confused he became, God's love was with him, unshakable.

His parents and that old man across the pasture had taught him that. God loved him. Period. And He was just waiting for Nash to wake up, admit his need for the Savior, and repent for turning away in the first place.

"Sorry, Father. Really, really sorry." He tilted his head back and watched the streaks of sun slowly spread in long fingers across the sky, pushing out the darkness.

God did that, too. Pushed out the darkness. Lit the path ahead. If a man was wise enough to let Him.

"Show me how to make this right. No matter what it costs me or what I have to do, lead me in the direction of Your choosing, not mine. I can't fix this, but I know You can."

Wrapped in the brightening rays of morning and renewed hope, Nash walked back to the house.

There, he poured a glass of milk and ate the rest of Harlow's cherry pie for breakfast. All of it.

His diet was shot to pieces anyway, so he might as well enjoy the pie.

After a long, sweat-producing workout and a good hour of shoulder rehab, he showered and dressed, eager to see Harlow again. She might not be eager to see him, but she wouldn't blast him in front of her grandpa or their son.

They had to hash things out. This time, he'd tread easier, reason with her, be clear that he would find a way to provide for her and Davis. He wouldn't let them down again.

Was that why she'd said no? Because she thought he'd fail her again?

Staring at his image reflected in the bathroom mirror, he rubbed a hand over the achy spot in his chest. *Davis*. He had a son. A terrific little cowpoke with the cutest dimple in his upper cheekbone.

He could barely wait to call Mom. She'd be shocked at first, but she'd also be delighted. She'd always wanted more kids. And she loved Harlow like a daughter.

He wished Dad was alive.

Outside, a vehicle engine broke the morning quiet.

His pulse leaped. "Harlow?"

Had she changed her mind about marrying him? Or was she here to hammer out visitation? Make demands? Work things out?

He hoped she wouldn't demand money.

At some point, he'd have his finances back in shape and no one would ever know what a fool he'd been. He didn't want Harlow thinking he didn't have sense enough to take care of her and their son.

What exactly *did* she want from him?

He'd give her anything he had.

Anything.

Tossing aside his comb, he hurried to the front door.

His stomach dropped into his sponsor-donated, overly expensive athletic shoes.

Car after vehicle, including a famous sports news truck, swarmed his yard, pulling onto the grass where they'd likely get stuck.

An eager-faced reporter bolted from the satellite truck and, followed by a guy with a giant camera, marched toward his porch.

How had they found him? He'd told no one.

Except Harlow and her family. And Ike Crowder. The old cowboy who'd boarded Drifter could care less. He barely knew Nash played professional sports.

An awful thought skittered through his brain and down his spine like a poisonous spider.

Had Harlow outed him on social media? Was this some kind of perverse retaliation on her part?

She wouldn't do that to him, would she?

A sneaky little voice nagged at the back of his brain. She'd never told him about his son. Four years passed and she'd never even tried. Not until he'd confronted her with his suspicion.

She hadn't wanted him to know.

Last night, Harlow had admitted the truth and then stormed away in anger.

If she'd done this to hurt him, she'd succeeded. And she must have.

Feeling sick inside, Nash Corbin, star athlete, plastered on his Madison Avenue smile and stepped out onto the concrete porch to greet his public.

He'd never felt this betrayed.

Chapter Fourteen

Finally. The well service truck rumbled into the Matheson yard to diagnose and hopefully repair the ailing water well.

Harlow, accompanied by everyone else in her family, greeted the two-man team, anxious for the verdict and for a healthy well.

Her head was muzzy and her neck ached from lack of sleep. Most of the night, she'd stared into the darkness, reliving the ugly scene with Nash.

The early morning sun nearly blinded her dry, aching eyes.

The TV meteorologist had promised a weather warm-up after the weeks of cold rain. Spring would eventually arrive and she, like all ranchers, was more than ready.

Except spring would most likely mean Nash had to report back to his team. As upset as she was about his ridiculous proposal, she couldn't bear the idea of not seeing him again. Now that he knew about Davis, there was no reason to avoid him.

She wanted him nearby, to see him every day.

She was still hurt by his proposal. But not hurt enough to want him to leave again.

What was she going to do about Nash Corbin?

Shoving her hands deep in her hoodie pouch, she sighed. She was hopeless, a romantic fool who couldn't let go of a dead dream.

Last night's confrontation had drained her. She'd come home exhausted and cranky. Storming into Monroe's bedroom, she'd spilled the entire, infuriating episode with the only person she could tell.

"So, marry him," Monroe had said with a nonchalant shrug.

Harlow rolled her eyes. "You don't even like him."

"But you do." Her sister, working at something on her computer, patted the bed next to her. "Harlow, you've loved that oversize galoot forever. You had his baby. So, marry him already."

Harlow plopped onto the quilt, a Navajo design in turquoise and brown. Monroe had a thing for Native American designs.

"I *love* him, Monroe. I want him to love me too, not marry me out of responsibility."

Her sister closed the laptop and set it to one side. She angled her body toward Harlow. "Is there any hope that he might eventually fall in love with you?"

"When he could have any woman he wanted? And probably does have a woman in Florida he would have to break up with to marry the mother of his son." Harlow shook her head. "No. He's not likely to fall for someone he hasn't even thought about in years. And that is not a marriage I want."

"Then, consider this." A sneaky grin slid over her sister's face, puckering the scars along the left side. "Marry him. Make him pay. Spend his money. Bleed him dry of every cent he and that agent robbed from us. Then, kick him to the curb." She tossed her hands into the air. "Win-win."

Harlow knew Monroe was joking. Sort of. "You're not helping."

"Okay. Okay. Don't give me that stink eye. Let's figure this out. You want him to have access to Davis, right?"

"A relationship. Yes. For Davis's sake."

"What else do you want?" Monroe waved off the question. "Beside the love thing. Which, honey, is way overrated. Trust me."

"You're too cynical."

"Truth. My objectivity went up in flames. Literally."

Harlow winced. As harsh as the statement sounded, the fire had done more than damage to Monroe's face and send her fiancé scurrying. It had scarred her soul.

A revved engine and clank of metal jerked Harlow's thoughts away from last night and back to the water well.

Situated in the backyard, the small, brick well house didn't contain space for everyone. With the door open so they could see inside, the Mathesons waited outside while the servicemen investigated the problem.

A new water well would cost them tens of thousands of dollars.

Please, Lord, she prayed silently. *Please let it be a simple fix that doesn't cost the earth. Not a new well. I can't afford that. The money from Mama's rings wasn't enough for a whole new well.*

"Low pressure," she heard one worker say.

Monroe and Harlow exchanged glances. Monroe rolled her eyes, her mouth twisting.

"Detective Sherlock says we have low pressure," Monroe muttered, dripping sarcasm. "Wonder why we buffoons didn't notice that our fauccts barely squirt enough water to fill a glass?"

Harlow elbowed her and shook her head. Her temples throbbed.

Monroe's bitterness sometimes seeped over onto anyone in her path.

Gus gave her *the look* and stuck his head inside the building to say, "Sure thank you boys for coming out today. Hope you didn't have any trouble on these muddy roads. Slicker than greased hog slop."

"No trouble." One of the workers, in thick brown coveralls and holding a pipe wrench, came to the door. "Saw a bunch of cars coming out this way though, making ruts everywhere. That'll be a mess until the road grader comes through again."

The comment flew past her. Cars drove down the road. The dirt road was muddy. No big deal.

But later, Harlow recalled the statement and understood its importance.

She was in the barn, finishing the chores she'd left this morning during the well service. The repair was more than expected but doable with the money from her mother's rings. Funds would be tighter than usual for a while, but with the small amount of Monroe's VA pension, the family wouldn't go without necessities. They'd get by.

Regardless of Monroe's advice, she'd never ask Nash for a dime.

Last night had rattled her to the core. She'd wanted him to know about Davis and was relieved he wasn't angry, but his ill-conceived proposal gutted her. Didn't he realize how humiliating that was?

Now that she was calmer, she'd meet with him today and find out what he wanted in the way of visitation. But she would never agree to a loveless marriage.

She still hadn't told Poppy that Nash was Davis's father, didn't know how she could. Another worry.

No wonder her head pounded until she felt queasy.

"Are you in here?"

Harlow jumped at the sound of Nash's voice.

Okay. Good. The mountain had come to her. No time like the present to figure things out.

Stepping out of the feed room, she went to meet him, resolved to keep a clearer head today no matter how tired she was.

The moment she saw him, she stopped dead in her tracks. This did not appear to be a promising start.

Dappled by sun-lit dust motes, Nash stood in the barn breezeway, hands on his hips.

Harlow skidded to a stop. The scent of dust and dried manure swirled into her nostrils.

Dark eyebrows yanked low, brow furrowed and body fairly quivering with fury, Nash looked like a supercell thunderstorm about to break. A tornadic outbreak that would leave destruction in its path.

He must be formidable on the football field. A random thought but there it was.

"Nash?" She tilted her head and inadvertently sloshed her throbbing brain.

Last night, he hadn't been angry at all. He certainly was now.

"What's going on?"

Jaw tight, he demanded, "We need to talk. Now. Alone."

"Okay." She held gloved hands out to each side. "We're as alone as it gets around here. What's wrong? Besides the obvious."

His eyes narrowed to slits. "I think you know."

She didn't. Her pulse banged against her temple, increasing the headache. And the anxiety.

Had he suddenly awakened this morning and decided to be mad because she hadn't told him about Davis?

"If this concerns Davis, I planned to meet with you today."

He slashed the air, cutting her off. "No."

"Then, clue me in. I don't know what you're talking about, if not Davis."

Nash scoffed in disbelief. His tan skin darkened with anger. "Don't tell me you had nothing to do with what happened at my house this morning."

Refusing to be intimidated by the big, furious athlete, Harlow parked a fist on either hip. "I have no idea what you're talking about, Nash. I've been here all morning with the well repair service guys."

"You didn't need to be at my place to cause the problem." He stabbed the air with a finger. "All you needed was an internet connection."

Harlow blinked, trying to make sense of his words. Was she too tired to think? Or had Nash lost his senses this morning?

What did an internet connection have to do with their son?

"Your revenge worked." Through a jaw tight enough to crack, he went on. "At the break of dawn this morning, I was overrun with media. A camera stuck in my face, photographer snapping shots of the ranch, invading my barn, my privacy, asking questions I don't want to answer. Can you really stand there and pretend you had nothing to do with that?"

Harlow's mouth dropped open. She splayed a hand across her chest. "Me? Why would you think I had anything to do with it?"

"Isn't the reason obvious?"

"No. Nash, no. I didn't tell anyone."

His hard expression didn't change. He clearly did not believe a word she spoke.

"Maybe you didn't say the words. But, according to several sources toting cameras and microphones, social media lit up last night with my whereabouts. So, maybe, after our chat, you logged in to your favorite platforms and mentioned to the whole world about lights on at the old Corbin Ranch, owned by none other than Nash Corbin, the NFL's missing player. Is that how you got the word out?"

"Nash, listen to me." Marching right up to him, Harlow gripped both his bulging biceps and gave them a shake. They were rock hard and trembling. "I did not alert anyone to your presence. Not by words or deed. I haven't had time to log on to social media in days. And, unlike some people, I keep my promises."

The last shot was intentional. But it was also hateful. She wished the words back but it was too late.

He jerked away from her, stacked his hands on

his hips and stared at the window lining the left side of the barn alley. His massive chest rose and fell in agitation, his breathing loud in the quiet barn.

"I needed this privacy, Harlow. My ranch was the only place on earth I could come without being bothered. Now everyone in the sports world knows its location."

Before she could check her thoughts, they tumbled out. "You signed up to be bothered when you pursued a career in pro athletics."

His gaze snapped back to her. His eyes narrowed. "That's what you think, isn't it? That I'm all about the attention?"

"Isn't it?" She was getting mad too. He had no business accusing her. Her voice rose. "Why else leave Florida without your phone and disappear without telling anywhere where you are? Why play Mr. Mysterious?"

She stopped, tossed both hands in the air. "You know what? Forget it. I don't need this. Your business is yours. It has nothing to do with me."

He leaned in closer, voice low and threatening. "It has everything to do with you. And my son. This is your idea of payback, plain and simple. Revenge."

She stuck her nose close to his. "You're not making any sense. Why would I want revenge?"

Nash pushed closer. She refused to budge. He would never hurt her, not physically anyway.

"You kept my son away from me for years. His entire *life*. When all you had to do was call. I was a phone call and a plane ride away. And now? I've been back for weeks and nothing. Not a word from you about my child. You kept silent until I forced the issue, Harlow. You, the control freak, wanted that boy all to yourself. I took away your control last night by demanding my rights, so you contacted the media. Did you tell them about Davis, too? That I'm the father of a little boy in Oklahoma? What's next? Selling your story to a TV reality show?"

Harlow gasped, wounded. Did he really think she'd stoop that low? That she'd hurt him or Davis that way?

She pressed a hand to either side of her head. Any minute now, her brain would blow up. "Stop. Just stop it. Let's be rational. We can discuss this like adults. In fact, I planned to come over later and discuss everything with you. But not while you're so upset."

"Upset doesn't begin to address my feelings right now. Not after this media invasion." He shoved a finger in her face. "But let me make this much clear. No matter what revenge you take, that boy is half mine. I'm going to be a part of his life, whether you like it or not. You can throw all the obstacles at me you want. All your devious efforts will get you is a summons to court."

Harlow sucked in half the musty air in the barn. The ugly threat ticked like a time bomb between them.

With deadly quiet, she asked, "What do you mean?"

"I mean custody. You want to fight?" He poked his own chest and enunciated every cruel word with precision. "I'm your opponent. And I play to win. You'll be hearing from my lawyer."

He spun around and stomped out of the barn, leaving Harlow shaking in her muddy boots. She reached for the wall to keep from falling.

Custody. He wanted to take Davis away from her? Because he thought she'd alerted the media?

Did he realize how little sense that made?

Or was his threat a culmination of things? She'd kept Davis a secret. She'd refused to satisfy Nash's wish to soothe his conscience and make amends with a loveless marriage. Now, the media had converged on him like a swarm of locusts.

And he blamed her.

So many reasons for him to despise and distrust her, even if he was wrong about one of them.

The shaking grew worse. She slid down the wall and dropped her face against upraised knees.

Nash was rich, powerful, famous. She was a penniless nobody with a failing ranch and a family to support. If he took her to court, he'd win.

She could lose Davis.

Raising her head, she stiffened her trembling shoulders.

She could not allow him to take her son away. No matter what she had to do.

Chapter Fifteen

Nash shut the front door as politely as possible, though he seethed with frustration at yet another invasion of his privacy.

Besides a carload of fans whom he'd sent away with autographs and a smile he didn't feel, a sports personality vlogger had hounded him until he'd given her a brief, taciturn interview.

The vlogger would probably roast him as a jerk.

Bad press bothered him. He was known as a good guy, Mr. Clean and Focused, always friendly to fans and the press, the guy who visited hospitals and charity events. Today, he didn't care.

If word of his financial collapse hit the news, which it apparently had yet to do, he'd be ruined anyway. Media would assume he had a drug or gambling problem. Even though the truth would eventually come out, the taint would remain.

He'd lose his reputation as well as endorsements.

Somehow he'd figure out a way to climb up again. He'd done it the first time. He'd do it again.

Once he settled the situation with Davis, he would hit the road. Head back to Florida and try to resolve the problems there. His peace and quiet was over anyway.

Harlow claimed innocence, but he struggled to believe her. How else would the media have found him? Monroe, maybe, but that would be on Harlow too. Good thing he hadn't told her about his financial collapse.

He did regret, however, his final outburst. He shouldn't have threatened a custody suit. Not only did he lack the money for such a battle, he didn't want bad blood between himself and the mother of his child. They'd have to work together for Davis's sake.

For Harlow's too, if he admitted the truth.

He'd caused Harlow enough heartache.

Even though he was upset about the media leak, he still cared about her.

He shouldn't have gone off half-cocked and loaded for bear.

If he could escape the relentless press, he'd go back to her ranch and apologize for that last, nasty jab, and try to work things out for the benefit of them both.

First, he had to calm down.

In the kitchen cabinet, he found a bottle of pain reliever and downed two capsules. His heart ached worse than his shoulder or head, but both throbbed after this morning. Another mess he'd made.

A knock sounded at the door.

The *back* door.

Had some reporter sneaked around to the rear of his home, unseen?

Anger shot through him.

Storming to door, he bellowed, "Go away."

"Nash?"

"Harlow?" He yanked the door open.

She raised both hands as if to ward off his fury. He felt like a jerk, seeing the angst on her face. "Please don't do this. Please. Can we talk like sensible adults?"

"Come on in." He stuck his head out the door and looked around. "Did anyone follow you?"

She brushed past him and entered the kitchen. "You sound like a spy movie."

Raking a hand over his hair, Nash managed a rueful grin. "They're driving me to distraction."

Harlow looked as if she'd been crying.

He blamed himself for that.

"Media? Fans?"

"Both." He shut the door and locked it.

"I came down the creek and through the back way to avoid them, but I didn't see anyone. How did you get rid of them?"

"Trust me. It's a temporary reprieve. I promised exclusives if they'd go away until I got back to Florida."

Harlow touched his shoulder. "Please don't talk about Davis to the press. Please."

Nash stiffened. "Your secret is safer with me than mine was with you."

"Nash, I did not—"

He cut her off. "Save it."

The timing was too perfect to be coincidence. He outed her. She outed him. Plain as the nose on her on face.

But he shouldn't have blasted her with a custody threat. He'd had time to pray and realized how wrong he'd been. He couldn't drag Harlow through court. No matter what she'd done.

"I changed my mind," she blurted.

"About?"

She drew in a deep breath and gulped. Pink tinged her cheeks. "Marrying you."

He waited two beats, blinked a couple of extra times. What had she just said? "Wait. Hold on. Say that again."

"I'll marry you. Today, tomorrow, whenever you say."

Eyes narrowed, he studied the woman before him. Last night, she'd demanded he never mention marriage again. This afternoon, she was ready to waltz down the aisle.

Everything in her posture cried surrender.

Something was very wrong with this scenario.

Sometime during his sleepless night, he'd decided she was right about his poorly considered proposal. He had feelings for Harlow, but a knee-jerk marriage could prove disastrous for them both.

"Why?"

She looked down at her hands. Her fingers twisted into knots. "Like you said last night, you are Davis's father and that gives you certain rights."

Something softened in his chest. As angry as he'd been about the media leak, he cared about this woman. *Cared*, a weak word for what his heart kept saying, but with the mess he was in, he'd keep his thoughts to himself.

Besides, something about her declaration seemed off-kilter.

"What about your, uh, nonnegotiable? Love."

Her cheeks reddened. She kept her eyes averted. "I—like you. That's enough."

It hadn't been last night.

What was going on in that head of hers?

A parade of thoughts marched through Nash's brain. Surprise, confusion, doubt. Suspicion.

Finally, awareness. The slow dawning that Harlow's proposal came with an ulterior motive. Something other than allowing him the privilege of openly becoming Davis's legal father.

He'd made plenty of mistakes lately, but he was not stupid.

Only a short time ago, he had threatened a court custody battle. Harlow adored her child. She'd do anything to avoid losing Davis.

Even marry a man she didn't love when love was her one nonnegotiable.

He got it now. Strangely enough, it hurt.

Harlow didn't want to marry him. She feared a custody battle.

"You want some coffee? Tea? Cocoa?"

She gave him a strange look. "Didn't you hear what I said?"

"I heard." He went to the kitchen counter and pulled out the coffee maker and began to fill it with fresh grounds. His thoughts raced with exactly how to handle this situation. Fighting was not the answer.

"Neither of us wins when we're angry. Let's have a cup of coffee and an honest discussion."

"I was afraid to come over here, but I couldn't leave things the way they were."

He didn't want her to be afraid, was ashamed of being the cause. "If anyone knocks on the door, pretend we're not here."

"I hid Burr in the barn."

"Thanks."

While he prepared the coffee maker, she pulled two thick mugs from the overhead cabinet and clunked them onto the countertop.

He liked having her in his house. Like old times. Compared to him, she was tiny. He'd always felt protective of her because of her smaller size. Still did, even though he'd failed her completely in the protection department.

God forgive me, he thought. He'd hurt her in so many ways. How could he ever make amends?

Instead of protecting her, he'd frightened her. She was so afraid that he'd take away her child that she'd offered to marry him.

How messed up was that?

Leaning his big frame and one elbow against the counter while the smell of brewing coffee filled the air, he watched her move around his kitchen. She knew where the spoons were kept, knew he had milk and creamer in the fridge.

Her long, cinnamon-colored ponytail swished softly against the back of her shirt. She'd shucked an old work jacket at the door.

He loved her hair, recalled how smooth and silky it felt against his fingers. If they married, he'd have carte blanche to touch it all he wanted.

As soon as the thought danced through his head, he squelched it. Harlow did not want to marry him. Not really.

"Let me ask you something," he said.

She imitated his posture and leaned next to him, her face turned to listen. "Okay."

Her eyes remained wary and her body tense.

He wanted no repeat of his morning's outburst. It only added to the tension between them and solved exactly nothing.

"If the idea of a custody battle was taken off the table," he asked, "would you still want to marry me?"

Her eyes widened, suspicious. "Is it?"

"Answer me first. If I promised never to even consider asking for custody, would you be standing here this afternoon, offering yourself as a sacrificial lamb?"

She crossed her arms over her chest and stared at the wall across the room.

Long seconds ticked by. Except for the drip of coffee, silence hummed on the air.

He knew the answer to his question, but he needed her to know it too.

The coffee gurgled to a stop. Ignoring it, Nash fixed his gaze on Harlow. He didn't want coffee any more than she did.

She bit her bottom lip, gnawed a little. Finally, she shook her head, her hazel eyes pleading with him to understand.

In a whisper, she said, "No."

The whisper might as well have been a gunshot.

Her answer hurt. Which was weird. And bewildering.

Some part of him had hoped for a different outcome.

Nodding, he said, "That's what I thought, so marriage is off the table."

"What about custody?" She gripped his shirtsleeve. "You can't take him from me. Please,

Nash. I'll do anything but give him up. Don't take my baby."

Fear made her tremble. That he was the cause shamed him.

He covered her hand with his, needing to calm the trembling. Her skin was cold. "This morning at your place, I spoke out of anger and frustration, Harlow. I didn't mean it. You are a terrific mother, raising a fine boy. A custody battle would hurt you both, and I don't want either of you hurt. Ever. I would never try to take him away."

Harlow wilted against the cabinets. Eyes closed, relieved breath loud in the quiet kitchen. "Thank you. Thank you."

When she looked at him again, he saw the moisture gathered there. Her tears shattered him.

Nash wanted to promise never to let anyone hurt her or Davis. Especially him. His selfish anger had cost her.

Harlow believed the worst of him, and yet she'd offered to marry him for the sake of their son.

A mother's love was a powerful force.

Instead of following his heart, which seemed all over the place these days, he patted the top of her hand and ached a little for all that was lost between them.

Could they ever get it back?

"I won't fight you for custody, Harlow, but I do want to know him and be part of his life. I'm a father. That's extremely important to me."

"I understand," she said, her voice still shaky. "And I agree. No custody battle. No marriage for the wrong reasons. Everything for Davis's sake. Okay?"

Why did he want to disagree, at least with the marriage portion? "Agreed. All I ask is to be his dad. Forgive me?"

"Of course." She managed a tremulous smile. "If you'll forgive me for keeping him a secret. I had my reasons, but I realize now that I was wrong. He needs you as much as he needs me."

"Thank you for that. I'll do my best to be a good father. Whatever the two of you need, I'll find a way to provide it."

Even if he had to start from the bottom and work his way up, or leave football completely and use his business degree, he would take care of his son. He would be the kind of dad his own father had been. "We'll figure this out, Harlow, and together, we'll make it work."

She pressed her lips together, watching his face as if she wasn't certain she could believe him. Another stab to his midsection.

"I promise, Harlow," he said. "Trust me."

Gradually, her shoulders relaxed. "Okay. Agreed. I want that, too."

He rotated toward her and finally allowed himself the long-desired hug. Nothing romantic. A hug between good friends coming to an agreement, declaring peace. A hug to let her know he never meant to hurt her. She was special.

Very special.

He heard the thought run through his mind and didn't fight it. Something was happening that he hadn't expected, but he couldn't do anything about it at present.

As if she, too, had longed to be close again and vanquish the awful disagreement, Harlow slid her arms around his waist and rested against his chest.

Nash found her long ponytail and smoothed the silky strands.

"This finally feels right," she whispered.

Though he didn't completely comprehend her meaning, he agreed. Harlow in his arms. He wanted to hold on and never let go.

Even if she'd alerted the press, she was still Harlow.

His.

Nash's mind stumbled over the possessive term.

"I didn't tell anyone that you're here, Nash," she murmured. "I wouldn't. Please believe me."

Did he? He wanted to. Needed to think that she cared about him enough to protect his privacy.

Moments, maybe minutes ticked by. He didn't care. Harlow's hands rubbed up and down his back. He enjoyed the soft rise and fall of her breathing.

He'd loved Harlow all his life. Friend love. But this felt different, stronger, richer. *Romantic*. Was he falling for the mother of his son?

Would that be such a bad thing?

Except Harlow didn't feel the same. She'd just said so.

Or had she?

She'd said love was nonnegotiable. She wouldn't marry without love.

He'd never been great at reading female subtext.

Relishing the softness of her cheek, Nash traced a finger along her jaw. When he reached her chin, he urged it upward with a knuckle. He wanted, needed, to look into her eyes. The green plaid shirt had turned them olive today.

Harlow tilted her head, expression soft and tender. Trusting. His promise had erased her fear.

Warmth spread through his chest. His pulse kicked up.

He couldn't give her much at present. But he could give her a man to trust.

"I really want to kiss you right now," he said softly, his voice surprisingly husky.

Her lips parted, curved. "I'm okay with that."

So he did, keeping it friendly at first. Then, Harlow tiptoed up and slid her arms around his neck, pulling him down. He bent lower, closer, his breath catching in his throat as he joined his lips to hers and tasted sweetness and heat.

His brain had been addled for weeks. Still was. One thing he knew for certain, though—he wanted Harlow in his life as much as he wanted his son.

He wasn't certain what that entailed, but he planned to find out.

Right now, he was in no position to do anything more than get acquainted with Davis. Furthering a relationship with Harlow was out of the question.

But he sure enjoyed kissing her.

Slowly, breath puffing as if he'd made a fifty-yard run, he released her and took a step back.

He shook his head, mostly to empty the wild thoughts of kissing Harlow until she agreed to run away to the preacher this very day.

Until he could get his professional and financial life back in order, he was right back where he'd been four years ago with nothing to offer anyone, especially his son and this woman he might be falling for.

Chapter Sixteen

Harlow's head spun as she stared at the man she'd loved forever. One minute, he kissed her as if his life depended on it, and the next, he backed away and poured a cup of coffee.

"Want coffee?" he asked, holding a cup in her direction.

She shook her head. The last thing she needed was another adrenaline burst. His kiss had rocketed her to the moon. What was going on in that brilliant head of his?

"What just happened?"

The corner of his mouth ticked up. Oh, that mouth. She wanted to kiss him again.

"I kissed you. And I'm pretty sure you kissed me back."

"I did," she admitted. "But why? I mean, why did you kiss me? Weren't we mad at each other a minute ago?"

Still holding out a mug, he looked at her for a

couple of beats as if he wasn't sure how to reply. Was he as befuddled as she was?

"Kissing and making up?" he asked, eyebrows raised.

She accepted the explanation and the coffee. Her hands trembled against the warmth. "Was that what that was?"

"Not completely. There's a lot going on in my life at present, Harlow. Things I can't talk about."

"Okay." But what did that have to do with kissing?

"If I had my way, I'd kiss you again. And again. You mean a lot to me."

"Because I'm Davis's mother?"

"Because you're Harlow, the girl I've cared about since we were little kids."

After that sizzling kiss, if he said *best friend* or *buddy*, she'd punch him in the nose.

"Friends with benefits, is that it?"

"No!" His forehead creased. He had the grace to look repulsed. "Don't even think that. I told you, there are major problems going on in my life. I don't want you or Davis involved in my junk."

"I'm a good listener if you'd like to talk about them."

"I know you are. I know. But this is…too personal."

Personal. As in his other woman. She wasn't a complete lamebrain.

"I'd say kissing is pretty personal, too." Especially that kiss.

He rubbed a hand over the back of his neck, mouth curved in a lopsided grin. "Yeah, it is. Should I apologize?"

She snorted, half-amused and half-annoyed. "You'd better not."

"Good, because I'm not sorry. Are you?"

Cheeks hot, Harlow gave her head a negative shake.

The only thing she was sorry about was that his kisses meant nothing to him. He probably had lots of practice.

They stood in his kitchen, each holding cups of coffee they didn't want, gazing at each other with an affection that simply would not go away.

How had she gone from resentment and fear to kissing in a few short hours? Was she going mad on top of every other problem in her life?

Maybe. But she loved this man, and he was going to be in her life. He might have other women, but there would never be anyone else for her. She might as well enjoy what she could.

A knock sounded. Nash's attention shifted from Harlow's pretty, blushing face to the living room. He put a finger across his lips. He was not talking to another reporter. Not today. They could knock all they wanted.

He was far more interested in the woman in

his house who'd suddenly become more than a childhood friend. He didn't know how it had happened, but he was glad, thrilled, shocked, fired-up.

His skin tingled to think about kissing her again, this time with full awareness that his reason had nothing to do with Davis and little to do with a guilty conscience.

The knock came again, louder this time, refusing to be ignored. "Nash Corbin, you old reprobate, if you're in there, let me in. It's Jonas Ringwald."

"Jonas?" They'd played football together in high school, had been good friends. Jonas had been with him the night he'd gotten the awful news that Dad had died of a sudden heart attack. His buddy and teammate hadn't left his side for two days.

Guilt slapped him. He had kept in touch with Jonas on social media but not as much as he should have.

"I'll go home." Harlow poured her untouched coffee in the sink. "You catch up with Jonas."

"Don't leave. We haven't finished our conversation."

"Was that what that was?"

He looked at her soft, curved lips and smiled.

Jonas pounded on the door again.

Nash pointed at Harlow. "Don't leave."

They had decisions to make. That's why she

was here in the first place. Not to addle his mind with sweet kisses. Except she had.

He and Harlow, also, needed time together to work out whatever was happening between them.

"Go," she said. "We'll talk later."

The knock came again. "Corbin, are you in there?"

Nash gave Harlow one last, apologetic look before heading to the door.

In four long strides, he wrenched it open.

"Jonas, get in here." They greeted each other with the usual male-to-male back slaps. He cast a quick glance over the other man's shoulder to be sure no one else lurked behind a bush, ready to jump out and snap photos. "What's going on?"

"I came to ask you the same thing. The whole town is abuzz. Our gridiron hero is back at the ranch."

Nash grimaced at the reference. He'd never liked being called a hero. Heroes were cops and firefighters, the military. Not grown men who played a game for a living. Sure, professional athletics was hard, punishing work, but not heroic.

"Word, apparently, is out." Nothing he could do about that now. He motioned toward the couch and chair. "I was hoping to keep a low profile for a while."

Jonas, a thin guy of average height with a shock of white-blond hair and laughing blue eyes, settled on the padded armchair. "Saw the injury happen on TV. How's it healing?"

Was that what people thought? He'd come home to heal the shoulder?

Better than everyone knowing the truth, that he was broke, had a son he hadn't known about and was trying to get his head together. Not to mention that he might be in love with Harlow, except his whole life was in too much of a mess to do anything about it.

"Coming along." Nash rotated the arm, thinking about Harlow. Had she left? "Would you excuse me for a minute? Be right back."

Leaving his guest, he hurried into the kitchen.

Harlow was gone. Nash wasn't surprised but he was disappointed.

With a sigh, and determined to see her later, he refreshed his coffee and poured a cup for Jonas.

Back in the living room, he set both mugs on the end table next to his visitor. "Still take it black, I hope."

Jonas nodded his thanks. "Any way I can get it."

"How are things with you and Krista?"

He'd missed the wedding, another regret. Jonas had married his high school sweetheart and settled in Sundown Valley.

"Krista's doing okay. Now. She's had some… health problems, but things are looking up."

"I'm sorry about the problems, Jonas. Really. She's a great gal."

"The best. Always doing stuff for others."

"I guess you have a houseful of kids by now." He couldn't seem to get the idea of kids out of his thoughts. Jonas would be a great dad.

Some of the cheer left his friend's face. "Still trying. No luck yet. We'd appreciate prayers, if you could spare them."

"Sure. You got 'em." Nash didn't know what else to say so he switched gears. He wasn't one for prying into a man's private business. "You never used those game tickets I sent you."

"Couldn't. Krista was in the hospital that weekend. But she's recovered and back to running half the town. She's the Chamber president now. Her latest project is the reason I'm here."

"Okay." If she wanted some autographed footballs for an auction, he'd get them. Or team jerseys. Whatever. Doing a favor for a friend like Jonas felt good.

"You know about Sundown Valley's Strawberry Festival, right?"

"They're still having that?"

"Bigger and better every year."

"That's great. I always enjoyed it. The carnival, all the different strawberry foods, the music, the rodeo." He flashed a grin. "Fun times."

"I'm glad to hear you say that because we'd like you to be our parade marshal."

"Me?" He was already shaking his head no. "I don't know, man. I have a lot going on right now."

Jonas leaned forward, his voice lowered. "Look, Nash, I've never asked you for a favor before, but this is important. Krista's gone through a lot in the last two years. A couple of miscarriages, a corrective surgery, fertility treatments, and still no baby. It's taken a toll on her emotionally."

"I'm sorry to hear that." Krista was the kind of girl who'd been on every committee in high school, the go-to girl. If something needed done, Krista was on it with a smile. If someone in school was sick, she rallied everyone into sending cards. She was one of the nice girls.

"Krista's thrown herself into this festival, and for the first time in months, the depression has lifted. She seems happy again. If she could score you as parade marshal…" He lifted his palms. "Well, I don't have to tell you how much that would mean. To the town and to Krista and me."

Nash needed to get back to Florida.

Conversely, he wanted a few days here to get better acquainted with his son.

However, the last thing he desired was to become the center of attention in Sundown Valley. So far, his agent hadn't made contact, and he'd like to keep it that way. Getting the upper hand was crucial. A leak to Sterling Dorsey that Nash suspected what was going on with his finances could eradicate any hope of regaining his fortune.

He could not afford for the unsettled details

of his private life to leak out the way his presence had.

But how did a man refuse a request like this one and still consider himself a friend?

Harlow drove Monroe to her doctor's appointment, hoping her sister would soon be free of the cast. While Monroe was inside the clinic, Harlow ran some errands, including a stop at the newspaper office.

Inside the old-fashioned brick building, she chatted across the long, wooden counter with the publisher and editor, Laurel Maxwell. The brainy blonde sported a gorgeous opal and diamond engagement ring.

Seeing the ring pinched the bruised spot in the center of Harlow's heart, a reminder of her mother's sold wedding set. But she was not about to rain on her friend's parade. An engagement was an event to celebrate.

"You're engaged!" Harlow pointed to the ring. "Who is the obviously brilliant guy?"

A slight blush crested Laurel's cheeks. "Yates Trudeau."

"Yates Trudeau of the stunning blue eyes."

Laurel's smile brightened. "My one and only."

"I read that article you wrote, about him being wounded in the military. How is he doing now?"

"Better every day. Thank you for asking."

"So, when's the big event?"

"We haven't set a date yet." Ever the newspaper woman, Laurel tapped the top of the counter. "I hear the exciting news that your neighbor is back at his ranch. Have you seen him?"

Before Harlow could stumble into such a loaded question, Tansy Winchell, Laurel's editorial assistant, poked her head out of an office. Purple color striped her brown hair.

"The dreamy Nash Corbin. My social media has been crazy with the news."

A frown wrinkled Harlow's face. It seemed the whole world was talking about him. Someone had leaked the news and it sure wasn't her.

"Nash has kept a really low profile at his ranch," Harlow said, "so I'm curious to know how his whereabouts ended up on social media. Do either of you know?"

"Easy one," Laurel said with a wave that stirred the fire in her opal ring. "Janetha Fanshaw. She and one of her teenage friends drove past Nash's ranch, saw him running through tires, and posted the news everywhere."

"They did?"

"Janetha's mom was in here this morning teasing me because her sixteen-year-old had scooped me on an exclusive." Laurel smiled, but Harlow saw the competitive spirit flash in her eyes. "I would love to interview him for the paper."

"He's still single, isn't he?" Tansy put in. "I'll interview him if he is."

Laurel laughed and shook her head at Tansy.

Tansy shrugged, unrepentant. "Well, is he?"

Heat crept up Harlow's neck. Nash's love life was not a conversation she wanted to have right now. The pair of them had a lot to work out, and until they'd told Poppy and Davis the news, she didn't want to say anything more about Nash to anyone.

He was still convinced she'd alerted the press. She hadn't, and now she had witnesses.

Nash owed her an apology, big time.

Thankfully, Laurel waved her assistant editor away and went right on talking. "Krista Ringwald stopped in earlier to buy a huge ad for the Strawberry Festival. Did you know Nash has agreed to be the parade marshal?"

Harlow's stomach soured.

So that's why Jonas Ringwald was at Nash's place this morning.

And Nash Corbin, famous athlete, wanted to be featured in the town event. She wasn't surprised, but she was disappointed. For all his protests to the contrary, he craved the adoration of his public.

What right did he have to be angry with her about the media leak when his ego needed constant stroking?

"His name should bring a lot of people into town," she managed to say.

"And revenue." Laurel's excitement was palpable. "Just having him back in Sundown Valley will sell a lot of papers, not to mention what will happen once we have an interview and photos."

"That's great, Laurel."

At least the town would benefit from Nash's inflated ego.

Taking a newspaper from the stack at the end of the counter, Harlow pushed her money toward the editor.

"Good talking to you, Laurel. Congratulations on the engagement."

She wiggled her fingers toward both women and left the newspaper office.

After yesterday morning's argument, followed by the most amazing afternoon kisses, Harlow's brain was too muddled to discuss Nash with anyone.

Nash spent the morning with Gus and Davis while also getting reacquainted with two of the Trudeau men as they righted the farm tractor, checked it over for damages and drove it back to the barn. Then, without being asked, Bowie and Wade Trudeau helped Nash load hay on the truck and feed the animals.

Considering the still-healing shoulder, he was more than grateful for the help. At the same time, he was thrilled to take this chore off Harlow's never-ending list. He wanted to surprise her, please her. After the chores, Gus invited the two ranchers, who were nearly as tall as Nash, inside for some of Monroe's chocolate chip cookies. With three big men, one wiry Gus, a chatty toddler and a well-mannered collie in the kitchen, the space was crowded with cheer and friendship.

Good neighbors. Nice men who were willing to lend a hand when needed. He'd let himself forget the positive things about small-town rural living.

Through drought and fire, storms and ice, and any other kind of trouble, friends and neighbors were there. When Dad died, he and Mom would have lost the ranch outright if not for the help and concern of their church and neighbors.

Real friends lent a hand when he needed them, not like the hangers-on in Florida who only used him. Most of those "new best friends" would disappear like wood smoke in a hurricane if he was no longer big man about town with pocketsful of money. Not all of them, but, he'd come to realize, an uncomfortable amount.

Something to consider as he sorted through his life in search of what really mattered.

One thing for sure, the Mathesons mattered, especially Harlow and Davis.

After Bowie and Wade departed, Nash had no more excuses for hanging around, but he couldn't bring himself to part from Davis. The boy had won his heart before he knew they were related. Now that he knew, Nash wanted to spend every possible moment getting to know him better. This was his baby, and he'd already missed so much.

He sat at the kitchen table with Davis on his lap. The boy had climbed aboard as if he somehow knew Nash loved him.

And he did.

How had it happened so quickly? Was there some secret in their DNA that bonded them?

A thick lump formed in Nash's throat. He cleared it, though the emotion didn't go away.

"You wanna play football?" he asked.

The cookie-crumbed face tilted toward Nash. "I don't got a ball."

"No ball of any kind?"

"I got a fire truck."

The kid needed a football to toss around. Or was he too small for that?

Nah, a boy was never too small to play ball.

In the future, he'd see that Davis had sports equipment, a basketball court, a T-ball game, plenty of football equipment. They'd have lots of dad-son time together.

Except Nash didn't have the money to buy anything right now.

And Davis would be here while he would be in Florida.

Somehow, he and Harlow must come to a meeting of the minds. Would she consider a permanent move to Florida?

Not likely. He couldn't even ask until he'd settled the problems with his agent. And his bank account.

Worries for another time. Right now, he wanted to enjoy his boy.

Since his son owned no sports equipment, Nash played fireman and race cars and Legos. When the weather proved sunny and warmer, he took Davis outside to play on the tire swing. The kid loved the thing.

Score one for the jock.

Gus, finally up and around, though using the cane more than before, sat on the porch and watched.

"Look at me, Poppy. Look. I go high."

Gus waved a weathered hand. "I see you, big boy."

Nash caught the swing ropes and leaned close to the sweet, dimple-cheeked face. "Want to spin?"

Hazel eyes lit up. "Yep! I gonna spin, Poppy."

"Hold tight."

Davis was a daredevil like his mama. The faster and higher, the better.

Nash twisted the tire and let go.

Davis's childish giggle erupted, spilling like silver glitter in the sunshine. Nash's chest swelled with love.

This was his boy. His son. He wanted to show the whole world what an amazing child he and Harlow had made.

How would she feel about that?

He glanced toward the old man on the porch. First, he had to tell Gus.

He wasn't sure how that would go.

"Girls are coming," Gus called from the porch and pointed toward the driveway.

Monroe's car stopped near the front of the house with Harlow in the driver's seat. Monroe exited the passenger side wearing a black walking cast. The hard, turquoise plaster cast was gone.

Ollie the collie raced toward her. She paused to scratch the golden head.

"I'm almost free!" she exclaimed, lifting the boot for all to see. "I can finally walk without crutches and get back to work."

"About time," Gus said. "You've lazed around long enough."

She clumped up onto the wooden porch and kissed her grandpa on the cheek. "A couple of weeks in the boot, doc says, and I'm good as new. I can even take it off to shower. What a relief!"

Monroe, who'd thus far treated Nash like pond scum, was actually smiling. Maybe not at him, but she seemed happy.

Harlow came around the front of the car toting shopping bags.

Nash stopped the swing ropes. "Let's go help your mom."

He lifted the boy from the tire and set him on the ground, then sprinted over to take the bags from Harlow.

"More in the car." She hitched her chin toward the Jeep.

"I help. I big." His short legs churning, Davis rushed to catch up.

With a squeeze in his chest, Nash handed his son a lightweight shopping bag. "Good job, Davis. You're a lot of help to your mother."

"Yep." Lugging the bag chest high as if it weighed as much as he did, Davis waddled toward the house.

With his arms as full as his heart, Nash followed as the group went inside. "Laurel Maxwell wants to interview you for the newspaper," Harlow said as she began putting away groceries. "She tells me you're the parade marshal for the Strawberry Festival. For someone who wanted to keep a low profile, that's a big change."

"Favor to a friend."

"I see."

He didn't think she did. Her mouth, that soft, kissable mouth, twisted up as if she'd tasted a sour pickle.

"What difference does it make now, Harlow? Word is out. I might as well do something worthwhile in the time I'm here." He reached in a bag and removed a jar of peanut butter. "It really is a favor for a friend."

She paused, one hand on a head of lettuce. "If you'll believe me, I'll believe you."

She still denied alerting the media. Had he misjudged her just as she'd misjudged him?

"The boy's right." Gus snitched a bag of chips

and opened them. Over the crinkle of plastic, he said, "Don't fuss at him."

"Yeah. Don't fuss at me." Nash patted his shirt-front. "I'm really a good guy underneath all these awesome muscles."

Snickering, she tossed a wadded shopping bag at him. "Bragger."

He laughed and rubbed the spot on his shoulder. "Wounded. You know you're not yourself when you're hungry. You want me to make you a sandwich?"

She grinned at his silliness. "This is my house."

"I can still make you a sandwich. Anyone else want one? I'm starved." Since recovering from the alligator in his guts, he couldn't get enough to eat.

"Me too." Acting big, Davis marched up beside him, his sweet face tilted back and up. "I help?"

Nash scooped the boy up in one arm and plopped him on the countertop. Harlow interrupted to make them both wash their hands. Bossy. But cute. Then they were back to work. Nash spread the peanut butter. Davis squirted grape jelly from a squeeze bottle.

Harlow punched him in arm.

"Hey! What was that for?"

"I learned something else from Laurel too."

He grimaced. Media again. Not his favorite people group. "Journalists are full of information."

"She certainly was, and this information had

to do with Janetha Fanshaw and you going viral on social media."

He frowned. "Do I know Janetha Fanshaw?"

"She knows you, as do most of the teenagers in this town." Harlow poked his good shoulder with the end of her pointer finger. "And she, not me, saw you running through those old tires and posted the big news on all her internet platforms."

"Oh." He blinked a couple of times as her words sank in. "She did?"

"Yes, *oh*, big guy. She did. If you don't believe me this time, call Laurel." She shoved her cell phone toward him.

Harlow was fired up, as she had a right to be.

Nash paused, a slice of bread in one hand, the smell of peanut butter circling his head and making his belly grumble.

Harlow really hadn't alerted the media.

He was thrilled that she was the person he'd first believed her to be. Delighted that the mother of his son was as trustworthy as ever.

He also wanted to pound his head against the wall in remorse.

He'd yelled at her, accused her, scared her half out of her mind.

Phoning Laurel Maxwell was unnecessary. Harlow was innocent.

"I guess I owe you an apology?" he asked, hoping this meant he could kiss her again real soon.

She sniffed, hands on hips, and a little haughty. "Groveling is my preference."

He added a second slice of bread to the sandwich and handed it to Davis. "Eat that, my man. It'll put hair on your chest."

Davis giggled. "Uh-uh."

"You're right." He winked as he lifted the boy from the counter to stand on his feet. "It won't, but it tastes amazing."

To Harlow, he said, "Talk to you outside for a minute?"

"For?"

"Groveling?"

"Public humiliation would be better, head in the stocks and throw rotten tomatoes, but okay, outside will do."

Nash grinned and walked her outside to begin his penitence.

The day of the parade arrived. Spring had finally come to the Kiamichi, turning the grass green and compelling forsythias and tulips to bloom. The hills and mountains went from patches of green pine and cedar to white dogwood and purple redbuds.

Spring was a busy time on the ranch. But Harlow loved it. Loved the warmth, the flowers, the cavorting baby calves. Spring smelled like hope to her. They'd made it through the winter, and the land would sustain them once more.

Even with all the work awaiting her attention, today the Strawberry Festival was a time to enjoy.

Nash had spent the previous three days participating in activities surrounding the festival. The town and plenty of state and local media swarmed Sundown Valley and fluttered around Nash Corbin like honeybees.

He smiled and shook hands and joked, basking in the attention as he used a permanent marker to scribble his name on anything and everything handed to him. They'd barely had time to share a strawberry smoothie.

At the moment, the three of them were at the head of the parade route, getting ready to begin. Bands warmed up, snare drums rat-a-tat-tatted. A tuba honked out a few notes. Horses pranced in line, their manes and tails brushed and braided with colorful ribbons. Last-minute adjustments to costumes and floats were made.

For the first time in years, Harlow had chosen not to ride Burr in the parade. Her focus was her son's first float ride. With his celebrity father.

Clinging to her hand, Davis, dressed in a miniature blue-and-orange football jersey and a team cap exactly like Nash's, was beside himself with excitement.

Nash, a head taller than the crowd and looking like the celebrity hc was, parted the Red Sea of fans and came toward her.

"Ready?" He held out a hand to Davis. Her son let go of her and grabbed on to his dad.

Nash looked at her and winked. She smiled back.

He surprised her by bending down for a quick, still-smiling kiss.

Cameras snapped. No doubt, she and Davis had just become the subjects of speculation.

She wasn't sure how she felt about that.

Nash lifted their son onto the float's giant, strawberry-shaped throne and held the boy on his lap. One strong arm looped around Davis's tiny waist, Nash leaned in to say something and point toward the carnival in the distance.

Davis eagerly nodded his head and grinned up at his father in hero adoration.

Tears threatened at the back of Harlow's eyes. Father and son had bonded faster and tighter than superglue. She couldn't deny or resent the love shining in Nash's face or in his actions. Davis needed and deserved this man in his life.

Nash had insisted they wait until he'd solved his problems in Florida—whatever they were—before they made any permanent arrangements concerning visitation or support. She'd assured him she wanted nothing, but he'd said Davis was his son, too, and he refused to be a deadbeat dad.

His insistence worried her some. Nash had mentioned taking Davis to Florida at some point.

She didn't like that. Didn't want her son out of her sight.

But if she fought Nash too hard, his money would win more than she could bear to lose.

Part of her didn't believe he would hurt her that way. Another part remembered the investment losses and feared the worst.

At her request, they still hadn't told Gus or Davis that Nash and Davis were father and son, although she had a feeling Poppy had already guessed.

No matter how private they tried to remain, after today, people would wonder.

Was she ready for that?

Leading the way with the color guard, the high school marching band began to pump out *Stars and Stripes Forever.* She spotted Yates Trudeau and his former military working dog proudly carrying the American flag. Because of his injuries, his gait was not the sharp, correct posture of a soldier, but he marched on, head high and dog prancing at his side.

The proud wounded warrior brought tears to her eyes.

Monroe had been invited to march in the color guard, too, but she'd refused, too self-conscious about her scars to be the center of attention.

Thinking of her sister's trauma brought more tears. Harlow blinked them away.

Slowly, Nash and Davis and their float moved into place.

Squeezing through the massive crowd, Harlow followed along, keeping her eyes on the man who held both her heart and her child.

The loudspeaker announced Nash as the parade marshal, promising more autographs and appearances throughout the day. The crowd erupted each time his name was mentioned.

An enormous burst of pride filled her.

When the parade ended, she reclaimed Davis and took him to the carnival rides. Nash was whisked away by festival officials to other events. He was smiling, but she noticed the emotion didn't reach his eyes. Craning his neck, he searched for her in the crowd and mouthed an apology.

He did that a lot lately.

He'd even hoped to escape his festival duties to spend time with her and Davis, but it didn't happen.

When the day pushed into evening, an exhausted Davis lost his cheer and Harlow took him home, more disappointed than was prudent.

Chapter Seventeen

Inside a small trailer near the football field, Nash enjoyed a plate of spicy barbecue brisket with coleslaw and pinto beans. The meal was the first break of any kind he'd had all day, and though he'd tried to find Harlow to join him, he'd been unsuccessful. He was disappointed that they'd had so little time together, but not surprised. Any time he agreed to a publicity event, he was swallowed up in demands on his time and person.

Still, he'd wanted to hold Harlow's hand and ride the Ferris wheel like old times. He'd wanted to kiss her in the dark spook house and then make her laugh by dunking the clown in the dunk tank. And he wanted to win her and Davis each a teddy bear at the football throw.

Simple pleasures, sweet memories. He wanted those things for her and Davis. Part of his penance, he thought, after realizing that he'd falsely accused her. But what he desired deep down was much more complicated than Ferris wheels and teddy bears.

He bit into a microwave-warmed dinner roll and listened to the man across from him rehash Nash's winning catch in a playoff game last year. The guy, Pete, an avid fan, had won a drawing to have dinner with him. Nash knew he was nothing without people like Pete and focused his attention on the man, even as he wished to be home with Harlow.

Home. Funny how the ranch he'd escaped was once again home in a way no place else had ever been.

Maybe because his son and Harlow were there.

"Mind if I get a photo with you?" Pete asked. "To show my kid?"

"Sure." Nash pushed his half-empty plate aside and stood next to the man while one of the festival organizers snapped the photo. "If your kid is here, bring him in for his own photo."

"Seriously? You don't mind?"

"Not at all."

The man scampered out the door faster than a jackrabbit.

Nash finished his meal, now cold but still filling. The man and two boys soon returned. He smiled and played his part, charming the boys while wishing for this to be over.

He signed a team cap for each boy and told them how much he appreciated their support for his team. They asked about other players and he regaled them with stories while the organizers snapped photo after photo.

When the happy trio departed, another man appeared in the opened doorway. A man in a thousand-dollar business suit and Italian leather shoes.

Nash's stomach dropped. His whole body tensed.

Sterling Dorsey, his agent, had found him.

"Nash, my man." Smiling as if he wasn't a cobra in the grass, Sterling said, "I've been trying to reach you. Is your phone broken?"

Guts clenching, Nash managed to keep a straight face and pretend a welcome he didn't feel.

"How ya doing, Sterling? What's up?" *Where's my money?*

"That's what I want to know. Why have you disappeared off the face of the earth? Do you know how far back in the boonies this place is? I had to rent a car over in Arkansas just to get here."

Nash ignored the condescending attitude. Sterling was a snob. An agent who was top-shelf all the way. His attitude had never bothered Nash until he discovered that Sterling's yacht, fancy parties, and half-dozen flashy cars were bought with clients' money far beyond his contractual percentage. Clients like him.

"Needed some R and R, someplace private while my shoulder heals."

"Fair enough, but I've been trying to reach you

for days. Business is booming, man. Have I got a deal for you."

For himself most likely. "What is it?"

Sterling pulled a chair to the small table and slid a twenty-dollar bill toward the festival volunteer.

"Say, hon," he said with a wink. "Get a couple of drinks for us. Keep the change. And take your time. Nash and I have business to discuss."

"She can stay," Nash said.

"That's okay, I don't mind." The volunteer took the money and left.

"Don't be rude to these people, Sterling. They're my friends."

"Was I rude? I gave the gal twenty bucks." He waved away Nash's concerns. "Little places like this don't matter anyway."

Nash fisted his hands, his tone flat. "They matter to me."

Sterling didn't seem to notice Nash's sudden tension. Or he didn't care. He had his own agenda. All Nash had to do was play along.

"How much did they pay you for this gig?"

Money. For Sterling, only the money mattered.

With a jolt, Nash realized he'd been no different.

"They didn't."

Sterling tsked, wagging his head as if Nash was a recalcitrant child. "Which is why you need me. So, listen up. Sponsors are clamoring for you again. You have become an even hotter commodity since your little disappearing act. A brilliant PR move, by the way."

Nash forced his fingers to relax. He had to think clearly and stay focused on getting his money back, not let Sterling push his buttons.

From his easy demeanor, the agent thought Nash remained clueless about the embezzled funds. If he was telling the truth about endorsements, Nash had a chance to recoup his fortune. At least, enough to take care of Harlow and Davis.

Working to appear casual and interested, he crossed his arms over his chest and leaned back in the chair. "I'm listening."

If legit endorsement deals were on the table, he'd take them. All of them. But this time he'd handle his own business affairs.

The next morning, Harlow finished preparing Davis's breakfast just as a sleek Mercedes pulled into the driveway and Nash stepped out of the passenger side.

"Nash. Nash!" Davis abandoned his toast and rushed out the door to slam into the big athlete's legs.

With one strong arm, Nash easily swung his son up for a hug.

They hadn't seen Nash at all since the end of the parade yesterday. Only a few hours had passed, and yet she'd missed him. So had Davis.

Harlow followed her son across the new grass, curious about the car. Something about its sudden, unexpected appearance gave her a bad feeling. This obviously wasn't a reporter or Nash wouldn't be in the car. Would he?

Was he about to leave town? Go back to Florida? They'd settled exactly nothing.

His actions of recent days said he felt more than friendship for her. His love for Davis was obvious.

But where did they go from there?

And what about the disaster he'd brought on her family? He still hadn't mentioned the pyramid scheme or offered an apology. He knew she struggled financially. And he must know the reason.

Why didn't he bring it up? Could he be that callous?

She didn't think so, and yet, he said nothing.

He behaved as if it never happened.

Something about the entire situation felt off to her. She desperately wanted to ask him about it, yet a part of her didn't want to know. Not now.

Not when she'd fallen in love with him even deeper than before. Not when she saw him as the same wonderful man, only rich and famous.

Nash was not the kind of person to hurt his friends without remorse.

Yet he had.

Was love so blind that she wanted to deny what she knew to be true?

"Harlow," he said, as she crossed the greening grass to the strange car. "Got a minute?"

Her stomach tightened, anxious. "Sure."

Nash hugged Davis a little tighter and kissed the top of his head before sliding him to the ground.

His gaze finding hers, he said, "I'm headed back to Florida."

"Today? Now?" Not now. Please not now. "But—"

He held up a stop sign hand. "I know. Unfinished business."

Davis stood at his knee, looking up with an earnest face. The expression twisted Harlow's heart.

"You come back?"

Nash swallowed hard and went to his haunches. "Yes, Davis. I will be back. As soon as I can." Gently, he pulled their son against his chest and held him there for a long moment. Finally, he cleared his throat and said, "I love you, little man. You be good for your mama, okay?"

"Okay."

Nash rose to his full six feet four inches. He dwarfed her. She'd always loved his impressive size compared to her diminutive frame. He'd made her feel protected.

At the moment, all she felt was vulnerable.

When Nash opened his arms, Harlow walked into them. He was her safe place…until he wasn't.

She wanted him to be again.

His giant heart thundered erratically against her ear.

"I'll be back," he said again.

"Promise?" She was afraid to trust his promises.

"I do. One way or the other, no matter what happens in Florida, I will come back here."

Right. He had to. His son was here.

The Mercedes window rolled down. "Got a plane to catch, Nash. Wrap it up."

A cold, empty expression shuttered Nash's face. He kissed her cheek and when she didn't move away, he kissed her lips.

Then, he let her go, got into the fancy car and left her standing in the breezy morning alone except for their child. Just like before.

Though the weather was pleasant, Harlow suddenly felt as cold as a January ice storm.

She'd seen the driver of the Mercedes. Nash had ridden away with his agent, the man who'd convinced Poppy to invest too much. All because of Nash Corbin.

The next couple of days were a whirlwind for Nash. He met with prospective sponsors and, although Sterling had urged him to sign immediately, he told every one of them that he'd get back to them ASAP.

The deals were good and with strong companies he didn't mind endorsing. He'd have to outwit Sterling to keep the man's grubby paws clear of the paychecks.

On day two, he contacted a highly recommended—and expensive—lawyer and set the wheels in motion to discover the truth behind his missing funds and an agent he knew was embezzling faster than he could earn.

The attorney advised him to temporarily freeze his financial accounts and fire Sterling. He'd already done the first. The second took some finesse and ego-smoothing, but he'd managed to get away without Sterling recognizing the true reasons. The agent would know soon enough when he was hit with a subpoena.

That night, exhausted from the round of stressful appointments, phone calls, and a long meeting with his coach and team owner, he retired to his condo. He'd agreed to begin rehab with the team therapists the next day. Tonight, he just wanted to talk to Harlow.

Only two days and he missed her so much his chest literally hurt. Did she miss him? Was she upset about his abrupt departure?

He'd seen the disappointment in her beautiful face. He knew he'd hurt her again. He seemed to be good at that. Would she forgive him once she understood all the things he hadn't been able to tell her before he left?

Opening his cell phone, he found her long-ago photo. Funny that he'd kept it all this time.

Or maybe not funny at all. Maybe his heart had always known what he was too busy to admit.

She'd looked like pure joy that day when he'd snapped this shot of her as she sat on the steps of his back porch, arms around her knees, discussing his dreams that were about to come true. His dreams. Not hers.

He knew she had dreams too, but his had always been the most important to her. She'd believed in him long before he'd become a success.

Harlow had loved him then, and he'd been too self-focused to notice. He believed—hoped—she still loved him, and the hope was like a hot air balloon filling his whole being with warmth and buoyance.

He wished she was here. Wished he'd brought her and Davis along. He'd take them to Disney World, SeaWorld, the ocean. Harlow had never seen the ocean.

He tapped her smiling photo and listened as the connection *brred* in his car.

"Nash, hi." Her voice washed over him like a warm shower, refreshing and pleasurable.

"Hey. How are things in Sundown Valley?"

"You're still the buzz. A couple of reporters stopped here today asking if we knew where you lived."

"Did you tell them?"

"Yes."

"Harlow!"

She laughed. “I told them Florida.”

He laughed, too, then. “Pretty smart.”

“We don’t want them roaming around our property any more than you do. They scare the cows.” He heard the smile in her voice.

“Everything okay with you and Davis?”

“We’re good. Are you getting your issues resolved?”

“Working on it. Listen to this, Harlow. I’m about to sign three very lucrative endorsement deals. TV ads, magazines, etcetera.”

“That’s great.”

All of a sudden, her voice sounded a little off.

“You don’t sound excited.”

“I am if you are. How long will you be there?”

So that was it. “I promised to return soon, Harlow. And I will. We left too much unfinished business between us.”

“When? Davis asks me every day. You made him love you, Nash. Please don’t abandon him. Please. He’s just an innocent child.”

Her plea cut through him, a saber to the bone. She still didn’t trust him. She might be in love with him, and he was convinced she was, but she expected him to let her—and Davis—down again.

Harlow took Davis horseback riding through the woods and along the flowing creek where she and Nash had spent hours as kids. Everything in this place reminded her of Nash.

He'd phoned three times since leaving and sent numerous text messages. He was headed to physical therapy. His shoulder was doing great. Docs said he'd play next season. Or he'd met with a sponsor and signed a television deal to advertise their insurance. Or he was off to have dinner with friends. They'd talk later.

That night he hadn't called. She'd been tempted to text him but hadn't.

Try as she might, she couldn't resist a look at his social media.

What she saw confirmed her worst fears.

Nash with a beautiful woman on his arm, smiling his million-dollar smile, and looking happier than he'd ever looked when he was here.

He had a glamourous life that didn't include her or Davis. But, as she'd suspected, included a very beautiful woman.

Her stomach cramped. She thought she might throw up.

She'd been a fool of the first order to believe she could ever win a man like Nash. He loved their son and was kind to her, but that was where the relationship began and ended.

He would never love her the way she'd loved him.

Nash was, in a word, miserable. Shockingly lonely for the ranch life, he did everything he could to clear up his business so he could grab a few days in Sundown Valley. He'd have to fly back to Florida sooner rather than later, but the need to go home was impossible to resist.

He had so much to tell Harlow. The phone was not the place to explain.

The lawyer had confirmed through a number of sources and a very sharp investigator that Sterling, indeed, had embezzled a huge amount of money from him, as well as other athletes. Micki Abelman, his new attorney, put things in motion to recoup what was possible, though Sterling was crafty and had moved much of it offshore. Nonetheless, the agent owned many possessions and had a healthy onshore account, as well as stocks and other investments to make him appear legit. Nash's lawyer quickly worked to freeze Sterling's accounts and file charges.

With the new sponsorships, Nash would eventually be all right. Rebuilding his portfolio would, however, require more time than usual because he already had plans for the first big endorsement advance.

Early Friday morning, he took a cab to the airport. He'd promised to be back by Tuesday to resume therapy and begin filming commercials for the insurance company, but he couldn't wait any longer to see Harlow and Davis.

Even a few days was better than a video call.

In the cab, he texted Harlow. Headed your way. See you soon.

She immediately sent a return text. Davis is eager to see you.

What about you?

There was a long wait. He arrived at the airport and exited the car, still waiting for her response as he rolled his duffel through the sliding doors and into the low hum of airport activity.

Finally, his phone chimed. See you when you get here.

Her reply was unsatisfactory but what did he expect? Neither of them had made any declarations of undying love.

Pocketing the cell phone, which he had the good sense to bring this time, he checked in and started through security.

A couple of fans noticed him and stopped for autographs.

After being scanned and his bag x-rayed, he sat down inside the terminal to put on his shoes.

His phone buzzed. He fished it from his pocket, glanced at the screen.

His attorney.

He held the device to his ear. "Hello."

"Mr. Corbin? Micki Abelman here." Brisk. To the point. Typical of this go-getter lawyer. "I only have a minute but I have disturbing news."

"That's not what I wanted to hear."

"We'll get Dorsey. This isn't that." Before he

had time to feel relief, the no-nonsense voice went on. "Our investigator discovered a pyramid scheme that your agent ran on unsuspecting victims with the usual untrue promise of a huge financial windfall."

Nash frowned. "I don't recall getting involved in anything like that."

"You didn't. He made sure you didn't know."

"Then what—"

"One of the victims was the family of the woman you told me about. The mother of your son."

Confidential attorney-client privilege meant he had discussed his plans to provide for Davis without concern that word would leak out and embarrass Harlow.

Finally admitting to himself that he wanted more than Davis felt good. He wanted the package deal.

"Are you saying he scammed the Matheson family?"

"Yes. Using your name to convince them it was legit. He claimed you had sent him."

A groan escaped Nash. His stomach churned, sick to realize how terribly Harlow and her family had been wronged by his thieving agent.

Through clenched teeth, he said, "If I get my hands on him—"

"Listen to me, Nash." Again, the tone was sharp and brisk. "As your lawyer, I strongly advise you to steer clear. Let justice do its work. I am very good at what I do, and I relish destroying creeps like him. Trust me. He will pay and pay big. You stay out of it."

Nash knew the advice was sensible but struggled to agree. After a moment, he said, "Fine. Just get him."

"I will. With pleasure."

"How bad did he hurt them? Give me the details. I have to fix this."

"You won't like it."

"Hit me."

Abelman sighed. "He bilked them out of basically every penny they had and what they could borrow. When the scheme crashed, they were forced to take out a second mortgage in order to keep their ranch."

His jaw tightened. His free hand clenched into a fist. He wanted to hit something. Someone.

Aware people milled around him, he lowered his voice. "How much?"

She named a sum that broke his heart.

Gus would never have fallen for a scam like that without Nash's name being involved.

It killed him to know how much he'd inadvertently hurt the people he loved.

Harlow had more than one reason to despise him. Except she didn't. Another reason to love her.

But now he understood why she'd been so cold

to him at first. Because of him and his association with Sterling Dorsey, Harlow and her family had been hurt terribly. Now he better understood the reason she worked so hard and worried about money constantly. And the reason she'd sold her mother's wedding rings.

Why hadn't she said something? Why hadn't Gus?

The call to board his flight broadcast over the intercom. He ended the phone call and, mind whirling, found his way onto the plane and settled in.

He would make this right with Harlow and her family.

Somehow.

Chapter Eighteen

When nightfall arrived and no Nash, Harlow sent him a text. He didn't reply.

Believing him to be in-flight or driving through the cell phone no-man's-land that these mountains could be, she tried to put him out of her thoughts.

Maybe she wouldn't see him until tomorrow.

Truth was, she was jittery, anxious. He'd sounded different in his one brief phone call during his layover in Atlanta. He claimed he had something important to talk to her about.

Was he anxious to establish visitation rights to Davis? Or worse, after consulting with an attorney, had he changed his mind about custody?

She squelched the worrisome thought. Nash wouldn't do that. They'd grown closer in the days before he left and even during their phone conversations. He'd made a promise and he would keep it.

She had to believe that or go out of her mind.

His final text before leaving Atlanta had even

ended with "Love." That's all. Just one word, but it was the word she'd longed to hear all her adult life.

Was that the important talk he wanted to have? That he loved her and Davis and wanted to be with them?

It couldn't be. She'd seen the photo of him with that beautiful brunette. Was Nash the kind of man to string her along as well as another woman?

She didn't want to believe it. She wanted to believe that he meant his text in the best way. That he loved her and no one else.

Maybe it was the friendship kind of love.

She thumped the heel of her hand against her forehead. She was driving herself nuts.

"Come on, buddy. Bedtime." She lifted Davis into her arms. "Ooh, you're getting to be a big boy."

The superhero pajamas she'd bought him last fall barely reached his ankles.

The ache in her chest throbbed. Her baby was growing up. He needed Nash.

So did she.

She read her son a bedtime story about Daniel in the Lions' Den. The Bible story was his favorite. He loved roaring like a lion and pretending to gnaw her arm until the angel of the Lord shut his mouth. Then, he'd pretend to be a nice lion and purr like a kitten.

So cute. At times like this, he reminded her of Taylor.

Once she'd settled her son, she flipped off the

light and went to her own bedroom to call her baby sister. A talk with her would take her mind off Nash.

Taylor answered, breathless and laughing. “Hi, sis. I’m fine. Stop worrying.”

“Where are you today?”

She laughed. “Hey, Shane, where are we?”

“Taylor!”

“I’m teasing, Harlow. Chill. We’re in New Orleans. You should see this place. The French Quarter is phenomenal.”

“We?”

She hedged, vague. “Just some friends. Is everybody at home okay?”

“Monroe got her cast off.”

“That’s great. How’s Poppy?”

“Missing you.”

“Don’t nag.”

“I’m not. I’m just reminding you that he’s not getting any younger.”

“Tell him I love him. Hug Davis for me. Gotta run. Kisses, kisses.” She made smooching noises.

“Taylor.”

The line buzzed in Harlow’s ear. Her free-spirted, unpredictable, and too-naive-to-be-on-her-own sister had hung up.

Pocketing the phone, she said a prayer for her sister, then peeked in on Davis. He was already fast asleep, so Harlow went downstairs to finish folding the laundry.

Mundane chores. No glamorous life for her. No night on the town, no fancy dinners or fancier cars. Unlike Nash.

Monroe sat on the couch, the laundry basket next to her, already folding while she watched an outrageous reality show. She claimed the people on the show were awful, which made her feel like a better person.

Harlow plopped beside her sister and began folding Davis's little shirts.

With the TV on, neither of them heard the car, but the next thing she knew, Nash stood at the front door.

In some impossible way, he'd grown handsomer and more dear than he'd been a few days ago. Nicely dressed in gray casual pants and an untucked, yellow button-down topped with a gray jacket, he looked every bit the successful man that he was.

Heart leaping like a kangaroo, Harlow pushed the door open. He came inside, and with a smile tugged her into his arms. She went willingly, hopefully. His cologne, so definitively Nash, invaded her senses. Expensive. Masculine. Alluring.

Tipping her chin up with a finger, he kissed her lightly. "Hi." And grinned into her face.

"Hi yourself." With Monroe right there staring at them, Harlow blushed as red as her hair. "You look happy."

"Happy to see you, upset about something else.

I need to talk to you." He included Monroe in his glance. "All of you. Where's Gus?"

"Probably back in his room watching *Gunsmoke* reruns." Monroe pushed aside a pile of towels and stood. "If this is important, I'll get him."

"It is. Very."

"You're being mysterious."

"Not my intention." He laid a file folder on the coffee table "I missed you so much. Is Davis already in bed?"

"Yes."

"Did you miss me?"

Like I'd miss my right arm. "I pined away like Juliet. You arrived just in time to save me from my dagger."

"Smart mouth."

She grinned at him, ridiculously glad to see him. Whenever Nash was present, her anxieties and questions seemed to slip away.

He leaned in and kissed her again as Gus and Monroe entered the room.

Smiling, he pulled her down next to him on the couch and waited for the other two to settle in chairs.

Then, the grin disappeared. Serious now, he flipped open the folder.

"It's come to my attention that a terrible wrong was done to this family. A wrong that appeared to be my doing. It wasn't. I had nothing to do with it."

Three Matheson faces, including Harlow's,

stared at him in silence, waiting for him to go on. They had promised to keep quiet about the investment scam and, unless he brought it up first, they would never say a word.

"When I returned to my ranch for the first time in four years, I told you that I needed to rest and rehab in privacy. That was true. But there were other reasons I came here, too."

"Go on," Gus said, his white mustache working as if he suspected what was about to be said.

"My agent—former agent—Sterling Dorsey, came to your home under false pretenses. He claimed I'd sent him with a financial deal guaranteed to set you up for life."

"You didn't?" Harlow shifted on the couch so that her knee touched his thigh and she could read his face.

"No. I would never knowingly involve you in something as shady as a pyramid scheme."

"Then why was he here? How did he know where to find us?"

Nash shifted his focus to her. "You know why, Harlow. Because of you. I was concerned about you."

She blushed again but nodded. "You can speak freely, Nash. They know about Davis. Monroe always knew."

"So did I," Poppy said gruffly. "Any fool knows my granddaughter only ever loved one man. She wouldn't be having someone else's baby."

"Why didn't you say something?" Nash directed his question to her grandfather.

"Wasn't my place. I knew God would handle it better than I ever could. Just like everything else."

"Your agent insinuated rather strongly that you were too busy and important for the likes of us," Harlow admitted. "But, he said, you were a good guy who cared about the little people."

Nash scowled, shocked, disgusted. "You know me better than that."

"I thought we did. But we didn't hear from you, only your representative. What were we to think? Success changes some people." As much as she'd ached, especially when she'd realized she was pregnant with Nash's child, Harlow had believed the agent. "The investment deal, as I saw it, was a payoff to keep us, meaning me, out of your new life."

Nash squeezed the bridge of his nose between his thumb and forefinger and shook his head.

"All lies, Harlow. Everything he told you was a lie. I sent him, but only to make sure you were all right. He claimed you were dating some guy and seemed very happy. You'd moved on."

"He told us the same about you and we believed him. I knew you wanted to escape this place, and you wanted a pro football career more than anything. I couldn't get in the way of that."

"What a mess." He sighed and closed his eyes

as if gathering his wits before he looked at her again. "I'm glad you finally know the truth. Do you believe me when I say I had nothing to do with Sterling's investment debacle?"

Gus answered before either she or Monroe could say a word. "We do. We'll say no more about that. And that's the word with the bark on it."

He tapped his cane on the floor good and hard to make the point.

"Not quite, Gus." Nash's hand found hers and pulled it against his knee. "I want everyone to know that Davis is my child, including him. Harlow and I will discuss those details later.

"And," he went on, "as humiliated as I am to share it, I want you to know everything else, too."

"You mean there's more? What a creep!" Monroe's mouth curled in distaste, puckering her scars.

"Monroe!" Gus's tone was sharp. He was a forgive and forget kind of man and would brook no rude behavior from his granddaughters.

"I'm talking about that worthless agent of his, Poppy, not Nash." To Nash, she said, "How did you get hooked up with such a lowlife?"

Nash's skin darkened in embarrassment. "That's what I keep asking myself. Me and about ten other athletes have the same question. Naive, green, eager, we thought this guy had our best interests at heart. He was smooth and smart, knew all the right people, all the ins and outs while we newer athletes were clueless. Besides, he was making a lot of money off us. Wouldn't he want to help us make more?" He blew out a disgusted huff. "Turns out, he made a lot more than he earned."

Harlow pressed her fingers against his, needing to console him. He'd been cheated too, big-time.

Nash squeezed her hand in return and then loosened his grip to lean forward, elbows on his knees. "Here's the situation as I understand it." He moved his gaze around the room from person to person until he focused on Gus. "Sterling asked you to invest in a deal, claiming I was involved, but I wasn't. I had no idea he'd contacted you other than to ask if Harlow was okay. My attorney only recently discovered the extent of the damage he did. Today, in fact."

"I thought you knew. All this time, I blamed you," Harlow said, heartsick that she'd believed the worst of the man she loved.

"We all did, except Poppy." Even Monroe appeared contrite.

"Blame don't help anyone, Monroe." Gus winked. "Prayer does."

"I'm sick that someone I trusted did this to people I care about. Sick and sorry and furious." With leashed strength, Nash bounced clasped hands against his handsome chin. "I will make it up to you. I promise. I *will* fix this."

"You don't owe us anything, son. I signed those papers of my own free will."

Nash shook his head. "Save your breath, Gus. We both know the truth now. I appreciate your kindness, even if I don't deserve it."

"Sure you do. You were scammed same as we were."

"At the moment, my finances are a mess, but my attorney is working to recoup some of my losses. The new endorsements will also help me get back on my feet."

Taking the manila folder from the coffee table, he handed it to Harlow. "Inside this folder is the first step in making things right."

Harlow opened the file and gaped in disbelief. "Nash. Poppy. This can't be."

Adrenaline jacked into her bloodstream. Heat climbed up her neck and scorched her face.

"Well, don't keep us in suspense. What is it?" Monroe impatiently leaned forward.

"The deed to our ranch." She looked back to Nash, incredulous. "He's paid off the bank loans."

"Both of them?" Monroe's tone was disbelief.

"Now, Nash boy, you didn't need to do that."

"Yes, I did, Gus, and we won't argue about this. I could never live with myself knowing that someone took everything you own because of your relationship with me. Because you *trusted* me."

"But you didn't steal the money," Poppy said.

"Doesn't matter." He tapped the folder. "It's done. Like a weight off my shoulders, I can do this and feel like a decent man again. Your ranch is free and clear."

Harlow shook her head. "We can't let you do that."

But oh, how she loved his good, good soul.

"Yes, you can. If not for yourselves, then for Davis's benefit."

When he put it like that, how could she argue? "I'm at a loss for words."

Nash's mouth curved. "That's a first."

Monroe snickered. Poppy chortled.

Nash stood, and Harlow thought he was about to take his leave. Instead, he took the file folder from her and handed it to Gus. "If the two of you will pardon us, we're going to take a walk. I need to talk to Harlow in private."

"Outside?" Harlow asked as he took her hands and tugged her to a stand. "It's dark."

Gus smoothed the ends of his mustache, a gleam in his eyes.

Monroe made a face at her. "Since when are you afraid of the dark?"

She wasn't. The only thing that scared her was the pain of having her heart broken all over again by this man.

"I'll protect you." Nash winked.

From the tender twinkle in his eyes, she didn't think heartbreak was on the agenda. At least not right this minute.

Ridiculously happy to feel his giant hand

wrapped around her fingers and relieved to know she didn't have to worry about losing her family's ranch ever again, Harlow followed him out the front door and across the porch. They said nothing until they began to walk. A full golden moon, nearly as bright as day, illuminated the shadowy pathway.

The cool spring night was beautiful.

"Where are we going?" she asked.

"My place."

"That's half a mile."

He shrugged. "Does it matter?"

"No. But I'm not waiting until we get there to learn what this is all about." The image of his other woman pressed in, warning her not to expect too much. "It's about you and me and Davis." He stopped at the gate leading to the open pasture. Instead of opening it, he leaned on the corner post and stared up the hill toward his house. "I have to be back in Florida on Tuesday. For a while, I'll be very busy."

Harlow tensed. She'd prepared for this, but she was still disappointed and embarrassed for dreaming of something more. "I understand."

"I don't think you do." He turned away from the corner post, his eyes gleaming in the moonlight. "I want you with me. You and Davis. Would you consider coming to Florida for a few days?"

Harlow glanced toward a huddle of cattle standing quietly in the field, shadowy silhouettes.

She wouldn't have to sell them now, thanks to Nash. She was grateful for that. "I don't understand. A vacation? Now? But you're busy."

"True. I am." He looked up at the night sky, his chest rising and falling in a sigh. A million stars glittered the inky heavens. "Everything's in turmoil right now. With the shoulder rehab, team responsibilities, dealing with the financial fiasco, and the new sponsorships, I absolutely have to be in Florida. But I want to be here."

"You never wanted to be here before."

"That was when I was young and a lot more self-focused, determined to make millions and never worry about money the way my parents had. The way you and your family have. But I've come to recognize the truth in the scripture. I'm not sure of the exact words, but it says something to the effect that it's no good if a man gains the whole world and loses his soul."

"You were never a bad man."

"Being bad or good isn't the point. I lost out with Jesus, putting money and football before Him and everything else that really mattered. I won't do that anymore."

"I'm happy for you, Nash. The only thing that kept us going over these past couple of years is our faith. Faith that, somehow, someway, God would work everything out for our good."

"I can't tell you how sorry, how regretful—"

She put two fingers against his lips. They were

warm and tempting. "Shh. No more apologies. I'm glad you found out what really happened and told us. Feeling angry and hurt toward someone we care about has been the hardest part. Worse than going broke. I never want to feel that way again."

"I never *want* you to feel that way again either. I want you happy and free of constant work and worry."

"Sounds good to me."

He took her hands and held them against his heart. "I need to know something. The truth, please. No hedging. From this point forward, I want the two of us to be open and honest. Can we do that?"

"I'd like that too. The way we once were."

"Only better." He lifted her fingers and kissed the tips. "Harlow, do you love me?"

"That's not a fair question." She tried to pull away. He held fast.

"No hedging, remember? If you love me, I want a future with you in any way we can make it happen. Here. In Florida. Or both."

Her pulse throbbed in her throat. She swallowed against it, afraid to hope too much. The vision of a brunette beauty haunted her. "Because of Davis?"

"Because of you." He let go of her fingers to cup her face in his huge hands. "I love you, Harlow. It's taken me forever to wake up and realize how much you mean to me, but I want you in my life. You and our son, together, as a family. But only if you feel the same."

Harlow loved his words, but she had to know for sure. "What about your girlfriend in Florida? Did you break up?"

He stepped back, arms falling to his sides. His chin dipped in bewilderment. "What girlfriend?"

"The elegantly dressed, beautiful brunette who looked like a fashion model." Her face heated. She was glad for the cover of darkness. "I saw your photo on social media."

Suddenly, his puzzled expression cleared.

"Spying on me, huh?" He sounded amused, the creep.

She punched his arm. "Don't make fun of me. How can you date her and then come here and say you love me?"

He caught her hands before she could whack him again. "Harlow, sweetheart, that wasn't a date. That brunette is my attorney. We had dinner to hash out a strategy for recouping my investments."

"Your attorney?" Was he serious? "Since when do attorneys look like that?"

He snorted. "Micki Abelman may be pretty, but she is a brilliant litigator who eats people like Sterling Dorsey for breakfast. She's one of the best attorneys in the business. Her only interest in me is putting another notch in the belt of her very successful law firm."

"Truly?"

"Since when did you become so insecure?"

"Since I had your baby all by myself."

Scrubbing a hand over his face, he groaned. "Can you ever forgive me? If I could go back in time, I would have been here every minute."

"And give up the dream you'd worked so hard for?" She shook her head. "You wouldn't have been happy, and I would never have forgiven myself for taking that opportunity from you. I refuse to regret the way things played out."

"Incredible woman. My best buddy and owner of my heart. Maybe I've done a poor job of letting you know, but I want you and only you. My brunette lawyer may be pretty, but she's kind of scary."

"Is that right? Scary like a man-eating shark?" Harlow knew he teased. She couldn't imagine him being afraid of anything.

"I prefer pretty, caring redheads in jeans and boots who drive too fast and can ride a horse better than me."

"I might know one of those. Want me to introduce you?" She slid her arms around his neck and tiptoed up so their lips were tantalizingly close, but not touching.

His warm breath brushed her skin, raising goose bumps.

"I've found her, if she'll have me."

"She's already yours, always was, always will be."

He wrapped his muscled arms around her waist

but dipped slightly away so that they were looking at each other, lit by moon and stars and cast in intriguing shadows.

"We have a lot of lost time to make up for."

Harlow's head spun in the most delicious manner. He loved her. He loved Davis. He was not the thieving jerk she'd thought him to be. And the elegant brunette was his attorney. She was almost delirious with joy.

Tenderly, she stroked his jawline, felt the soft scruff of his long, very busy day. "Nash Corbin, I've loved you all my life."

He gazed into her eyes with such sweet tenderness, her knees trembled.

"Will you love me, and let me love you, all the rest of it?"

"Is this a proposal? This better be a real proposal this time." She narrowed her eyes, partially teasing but serious too. "Because I'm not ever coming to Florida with you unless it is."

His teeth flashed.

"It is." He dropped his hold and fumbled inside his jacket. "Almost forget something very important."

"What could be more important than a marriage proposal?"

"This." He extracted a box from his pocket and flipped open the lid. Inside was a set of rings. Even in the moonlight, they sparkled.

Harlow gasped. Tears sprang to her eyes. Any

residual doubt she had flew off into the Milky Way. "My mother's wedding rings. How did you— When did you— Oh, Nash."

"I paid the ransom," he said, with a pleased smile.

"You don't know how much this means to me."

"Yes, I do. Remember? I held you while you cried. It about broke my heart. I badly wanted to take care of the mortgage, the well repair, everything, right then, but I couldn't. That's when I realized I was falling in love with you, that I wanted to take care of you forever and never see you cry again."

"Why didn't you tell me?"

"Pride, I guess, after my financial missteps. Fear that I'd never be the man, the provider, you and Davis deserve." He rubbed his fingers over the engagement stone. "Do you like these? Would you rather choose your own?"

"No. These are perfect. You knew they'd be perfect." A tear slipped down her cheek as she extended her hand to him.

"I was hoping," he said. "Now, let's make this official."

With the cattle moving softly and the stars twinkling overhead, he went to one knee right there on the dew-damp grass. "Will you, Harlow Matheson, woman I adore and mother of my beautiful son, marry me even if I'm broke, both financially and physically?"

"Temporarily broke," she corrected. "Your shoulder will heal, and no unscrupulous agent will keep you from being a financial and professional success. But if neither happened, I'd still love you."

His lips curved. "You always believed in me, even when you thought the worst."

"Love does that, I think."

"So, will you marry me?"

"Yes. Yes! Of course, I will."

Eyes gleaming with happiness as they looked into hers, Nash slid her mother's engagement ring onto her left ring finger.

With a half laugh, half sob, Harlow fell against his big, hard-muscled, athletic body and buried her wet face against his warm neck. He caught her easily, never giving an inch, holding her secure, the way he'd promised to do from now on.

"Are you crying?" His own voice sounded husky and choked.

"No." She sobbed into his shoulder. "I'm happy."

A soft laugh rumbled in his chest. "Me, too."

Epilogue

Valentine's Day had never been Harlow's favorite holiday, but it was now and always would be. So much had happened in less than a year, and at last, she and Nash had come to this perfect day.

Never mind that winter hung on with cold fingers, and shiny gray clouds obliterated the sun. Their love would light up the world.

"Get a move on, sister." As maid of honor, Monroe looked resplendent in a sleek, red, one-shouldered gown and the highest heels Harlow had ever seen her wear. With her blond hair clipped up on one side and the other side swooped over her scarred cheek, she looked like a 1940s screen star. "If you're determined to marry him, the big oaf is waiting."

Harlow slid her mother's earrings, borrowed from Monroe, into her earlobes. Something old and new, borrowed and blue, she'd kept to the fun, old traditions. "You like him."

"Put it this way. As long he keeps treating you like royalty, I won't break his kneecaps."

Bubbling with joy, Harlow hugged her sister. Tough girl had finally succumbed to Nash's charm and natural kindness. "He really is a good guy."

"I guess. If there is such a thing." Monroe smiled to show she teased and leaned in to kiss Harlow's cheek. "You are so gorgeous in that dress. He's going to collapse when he sees you. Or cry." She rubbed her hands together. "I love seeing big men cry."

"Not too froufrou?" Harlow stroked her hands over the tulip skirt. She felt like a fairy princess in the long, lacy, winter-white gown and strappy heels. Everything about their wedding felt surreal.

In homage to Valentine's Day, pink and white with splashes of red were their wedding colors. Nash claimed he didn't care one way or the other because his tux was black, his shirt white and he'd wear whatever tie she liked. She'd chosen red.

"Perfect. It's you."

Harlow scoffed. "Muddy boots and faded jeans are me. This is like a dream. A fantasy. A fairy tale."

"That's the way weddings are supposed to be." Monroe arched a cynical, if perfectly groomed, eyebrow. "Or so I'm told."

If anyone was gorgeous it was Monroe, although such fancy attire was as unusual for the navy veteran as it was for Harlow.

"Mama." Davis sprawled on his belly on a small sofa watching cartoons on Harlow's phone. "Can we go now?"

He was getting restless, but so was she.

The now four-year-old had wanted to wear his football jersey, but Nash had convinced him that they should dress alike. The little boy adored his newfound daddy, so the deal was done. Nash had even taken him shopping, proudly showing off his son to anyone who noticed.

Some mornings Harlow woke up and pinched herself, wondering if she'd dreamed the past year.

The only thing that would have made today better was if Taylor was here as a bridesmaid. Harlow had asked, had even sent the bridesmaid dress. At first, Taylor had agreed. Then, she'd changed her mercurial mind without even making up an excuse. She couldn't make it. Sorry. Shoot her a video of the ceremony.

The hurt from that rejection still stung, but Harlow refused to let it ruin her day. Taylor was different. Always had been. She'd had some struggles in high school. Since then, she was like an autumn wind—no one could predict which way she'd blow.

"I could kick her behind," Monroe said, as if reading Harlow's thoughts. "She should be here."

"Never mind. Today is beautiful anyway."

Giving herself one more glance in the mirror, she adjusted the sparkling jeweled headband, checked the back of her long, curled hair, then nodded. “I’m ready.”

Davis hopped to his feet. “Is Dad here?”

“He better be,” Monroe muttered.

“Yes, he’s waiting for us.” Harlow squatted, her long dress swishing against the tile. “Here, let me fix your tie. It’s crooked.”

The four-year-old tilted his neck to give her access. “Can we eat cake now?”

“Soon.” She patted his chest, hugged him. “All done. Where’s Poppy?”

“Coming.” Monroe hitched her chin toward the hallway as she guided Davis and Harlow’s bridesmaids out the door to line up for the processional.

Poppy appeared in their place. Determined to walk her down the aisle without using his cane, he wore braces on both knees beneath his black trousers.

She was so proud to be the granddaughter of this fine old gentleman, who once had cowboyed on the biggest spreads in Texas. As raw and solid as the earth, this man had been her anchor in every storm.

When Gus’s eyes found her, moisture filled them. He blinked it away, cleared his throat. Cowboys didn’t cry, he’d say. But she knew better.

“You gussied up real good, sis. Pretty as a paint mare.”

From Poppy, that was high praise.

"I love you, Poppy. Thank you for raising me when you didn't have to, for loving me, for teaching me about Jesus and so many other good things. You really are the best."

He sniffed. His snowy mustache quivered.

"Yep. Well. I love you too." He cleared his throat and nodded. "Let's get this show on the road."

Harlow kissed his weathered cheek, hooked her hand over his elbow and went out to meet her groom.

Nash adjusted his red tie for the tenth time. He was as fidgety as a rookie in his first NFL game. Not because he harbored a single doubt. Not because there were a hundred close friends and family filing into the small-town church.

In a few minutes, he'd marry the woman of his heart and the mother of his son. He'd never felt such eagerness, not even on the football field.

Zack and Jonas, along with Aaron, his third groomsman, another teammate, milled around the dressing room, cracking jokes and razzing each other. The two muscular football players had taken an immediate liking to the much smaller Jonas. Fine men he was proud to share this special day with.

Nash's shoulder had healed well, and he'd enjoyed a successful season of play. Even though his team hadn't made it out of the playoffs this year, his stats were strong, his team happy and his contract lucrative.

Best of all, Sterling Dorsey was in jail. Although too much of Nash's money was long gone, his go-getter attorney had recouped a healthy sum, and Nash was now fully in charge of his own finances.

He could finally support his son and his bride in the manner they deserved.

Life was good. Today it got better.

Today, he gained a wife and officially became a father to his son. He hadn't yet won another championship, but he'd won the best two prizes a man could have.

Throughout the football season, Harlow and Davis had flown back and forth to Florida, making the separation more tolerable. He'd taken great delight in squiring them around, introducing them, and in showing them the many wonderful amenities Florida had to offer. After visiting SeaWorld, Davis had declared he wanted to be a dolphin man when he grew up. And a football player like his dad.

In true Harlow style, she wanted Sundown Valley to be their home base with Florida as a second home. She loved them both but refused to permanently leave her eighty-one-year-old grandfather. How could a man argue with such devotion?

City or country, if she was there, he'd be fulfilled. For a man who'd once wanted to escape the stresses of ranching, he'd learned the value of true friendships and of appreciating his roots.

He'd also learned to put his trust in God instead of money, a hard lesson, but one he planned to teach his son. God first, everything else second, guaranteed that life would always work out for the good.

Pastor Cloud stuck his head inside the room. "Time to go, boys."

His heart jumped.

Unable to stop the smile plastered on his face, Nash exited the anteroom with his three best pals.

Mom was here somewhere with husband Danny, all the way from Ireland. She'd been ecstatic to meet her grandson of the matching dimple and thrilled that her son had finally opened his eyes and his heart to the girl next door who'd always adored him.

Women were so smart.

As he and his attendants filed into place in front of the church next to Pastor Cloud, a lone pianist trilled gentle hymns.

And then it happened. The music changed. The heart-gripping wedding march began.

His adrenaline jacked high enough to run a hundred-yard dash with eleven big guys chasing him.

He thought his bounding heart might crack his

rib cage when, like a trumpet blast to his soul, Harlow appeared at the top of the aisle.

He'd heard about these moments, had considered them to be the result of some writer's imagination.

He'd been wrong.

Every cell in his body exploded with joy.

Like the photographer snapping away, his mind captured every detail of his bride.

With Gus straight and proud beside her, Harlow was a vision in white, carrying a bouquet of red, pink and white roses. Her long cinnamon-colored hair curled over one shoulder. Diamonds dangled from her ears, catching the light.

He'd always heard that a bride in love glowed. He'd never believed it until now. Did he have that same rapturous expression on his face?

He suspected he did.

The next moments seemed to move on fast-forward, and yet, were suspended in time. Acutely aware of every word and action, he hid them in his heart to revisit with Harlow later. Was she feeling the same ecstatic joy? Did she notice that everyone in the building was smiling, and some, like his mother, through tears?

The ancient words were spoken, rings exchanged, and suddenly he was a husband.

"Nash, you may kiss your bride."

"Gladly." Harlow raised her blushing face to

his and he bent her backward, kissed her soundly and laughed into her eyes. "I love you."

"You better." Her moist lips curved. She pulled his head down for another kiss. A ripple of laughter moved through the congregation.

As he set her back on her feet, a small body slammed into his legs. He swooped his son into his arms.

Then, for the entire church to hear, Davis asked, "Is this over? Can we eat cake now?"

As a second wave of laughter filtered through the church and cameras snapped and filmed, Harlow lifted her bouquet high into the air and declared, "Let them eat cake!"

Inside the church fellowship hall, the reception was in full swing when it happened. Two things, actually, that Harlow would forever hold in her heart as icing on an already beautiful wedding day.

Music played through the sound system. The scent of reception foods mingled with the fragrance of roses. A crowd of well-wishers filled tables and milled about, visiting with friends most of them had known forever. If some were starstruck by Nash and his friends, they maintained their Southern manners well enough not be an embarrassment.

Harlow held on to her husband's hand as they prepared to cut the fancy, flowery wedding cake.

The photographer snapped photo after photo. Laurel Maxwell, who'd been given permission to write an article for the newspaper, snapped a few, as well, a lean and handsome Yates Trudeau at her side.

At the exact moment Harlow and Nash sliced into the cake, the outer glass doors swung open. A swirl of cold snaked across the floor.

"Look," someone cried. "It's snowing."

Harlow glanced up, the cake momentarily forgotten. Her heart leaped. Her soul sang. She hadn't known she could be any happier than she already was.

For indeed, fluffy fat white flakes floated from the sky like dove feathers pouring from heaven. But it wasn't the perfectly timed snow that held her attention.

Dappled in that beautiful white blessing was a breathless, smiling, dark-haired woman in a pink bridesmaid dress. Late, but finally here.

"Taylor." Harlow's chest squeezed.

Nash leaned close to her ear. "Look what the snow blew in."

She heard the smile in his voice. "You did this."

"A wedding present. To make your day perfect. Though I can't take credit for the snow."

She turned to face him, then, and with all the love she'd carried for years, touched his jaw and smiled. "Thank you."

"Let's go say hello."

Cake left with the servers, Nash took her hand in his giant paw and cleared a path to her sister.

Cleared a path. That's what he'd done to bring them together as a family. All of them. Even the wayward sister.

Since that precious night when he'd redeemed her mother's rings and she'd agreed to marry him, Nash had done everything in his power to make up for lost time with her and their son.

Harlow knew, if she hadn't known before, that his was a love worth finding, a love worth waiting for.

A love that would last forever.

* * * * *

Don't miss the next book in New York Times *bestselling author Linda Goodnight's Sundown Valley miniseries coming soon!*

And look for the previous titles in the series:

To Protect His Children
Keeping Them Safe
The Cowboy's Journey Home

Available now wherever Love Inspired books are sold!